KU-637-429

**'I won't let you down.' She raised her chin in a businesslike manner and assumed a look she prayed was professional. 'When would you like me to start?'**

'We'll discuss the details over dinner. Including salary,' he said gently.

The reminder that she hadn't even asked the basics before accepting the position brought a telltale colour to her cheeks, but this time she didn't falter. 'I've always adhered to the idea you get what you are prepared to pay for in this world.'

'Is that so?' he said silkily, his eyes intent on her flushed face. 'Then I hope your salary buys everything I need from you, Toni...'

**Helen Brooks** lives in Northamptonshire, and is married with three children and three beautiful grandchildren. As she is a committed Christian, busy housewife, mother and grandma, her spare time is at a premium, but her hobbies include reading, swimming and gardening, and walks with her husband and their two Irish terriers. Her long-cherished aspiration to write became a reality when she put pen to paper on reaching the age of forty and sent the result off to Mills & Boon®.

**Recent titles by the same author:**

SNOWBOUND SEDUCTION
SWEET SURRENDER WITH THE MILLIONAIRE
THE MILLIONAIRE'S CHRISTMAS WIFE
THE BOSS'S INEXPERIENCED SECRETARY

# THE BEAUTIFUL WIDOW

BY
HELEN BROOKS

MILLS
BOON

All the characters in this book have no existence outside the imagination of the author, and have no relation whatsoever to anyone bearing the same name or names. They are not even distantly inspired by any individual known or unknown to the author, and all the incidents are pure invention.

All Rights Reserved including the right of reproduction in whole or in part in any form. This edition is published by arrangement with Harlequin Enterprises II BV/S.à.r.l. The text of this publication or any part thereof may not be reproduced or transmitted in any form or by any means, electronic or mechanical, including photocopying, recording, storage in an information retrieval system, or otherwise, without the written permission of the publisher.

® and TM are trademarks owned and used by the trademark owner and/or its licensee. Trademarks marked with ® are registered with the United Kingdom Patent Office and/or the Office for Harmonisation in the Internal Market and in other countries.

First published in Great Britain 2011
by Mills & Boon, an imprint of Harlequin (UK) Limited,
Eton House, 18-24 Paradise Road, Richmond, Surrey TW9 1SR

© Helen Brooks 2011

ISBN: 978 0 263 22004 9

Harlequin (UK) policy is to use papers that are natural, renewable and recyclable products and made from wood grown in sustainable forests. The logging and manufacturing process conform to the legal environmental regulations of the country of origin.

Printed and bound in Great Britain
by CPI Antony Rowe, Chippenham, Wiltshire

# THE BEAUTIFUL WIDOW

| MORAY COUNCIL LIBRARIES & INFO.SERVICES | |
| --- | --- |
| 20 31 97 82 | |
| **Askews & Holts** | |
| RF RF | |
| | |

# CHAPTER ONE

STEEL LANDRY WAS running out of patience. A man who suffered fools badly, he'd spent most of the morning sorting out what he termed as a 'pig's ear' of a mess. Since his property business had mushroomed into a multimillion-pound operation with tentacles reaching into a dozen major cities in the UK, out of necessity he'd been forced to rely on the personnel he employed in the various offices he had all over the country. He couldn't be everywhere at once—much as he would have liked to have been. And one of his managers had let him down badly, ignoring contractual obligations and placing the name of Landry Enterprises in disrepute. The morning had been a damage control exercise and although the matter was now resolved it had left a nasty taste in his mouth. Add to that the fact he hadn't slept well the night before—his brother-in-law had phoned an hour ago to say Steel's sister was in hospital with a threatened miscarriage, and his very able and reliable secretary had given in her notice due to her husband's job moving to the States—and it summed up the perfect Monday.

He glared at the smoked salmon sandwiches his secretary had fetched for his lunch and called the hospital for the second time in twenty minutes. The answer was still the same: Mrs Wood was as comfortable as could be expected, which in hospital jargon probably meant she was suffering the torments of the damned.

As soon as Jeff, his brother-in-law, had phoned, Steel had contacted the hospital and arranged for a private room and the top consultant. Now he resolved he'd put all further business for the day on hold and go across London to the hospital himself to make sure Annie was having the best treatment available. Jeff was a great guy and devoted to Annie, but a typical high-brow academic who was so absorbed in his job as an astronomer, researching satellite communication systems and space agency work at a top avionic company, that he barely saw what was in front of him on planet earth.

Decision made, he checked his diary. Nothing that couldn't wait. And then he frowned. Although there was that woman he was interviewing at the end of the day for the post of interior designer, the one James had personally recommended. What was her name? Oh, yeah, Toni George. He glanced at the gold Rolex on one tanned wrist. Getting on for three o'clock, and Mrs George was due to arrive at five-thirty.

Steel flexed his muscled shoulders, rotating his head to ease the tension in his neck. The hospital was only a stone's throw from his apartment; he didn't particularly fancy battling back to the office after he'd left there only to retrace the journey once the interview was over. Flicking the switch on the intercom on his desk, he said, 'Joy, this interview later with Toni George. See if you can contact her and arrange for her to call at my apartment instead of here. I'm going to be leaving the hospital about that time. Do it now, would you?'

Less than two minutes later his secretary tapped on the door and put her sleek blonde head into the room. 'All arranged,' she said briskly, 'although I did mention you were visiting your sister in hospital close to your apartment when she seemed a little...wary about the change of location. She was fine after that.'

He surveyed Joy through amused eyes. He hadn't thought this Mrs George might think he had ulterior motives; perhaps he should have. Reaching for his suit jacket on the back of his chair, he stood up. 'Thanks,' he said briefly. 'Oh, and give Stuart my congratulations on the promotion.'

'Will do.' Joy regarded him sympathetically. She knew Steel thought the world of his sister and this news had knocked him for six, although as ever the hard, handsome face showed little emotion. She had worked for him for four years and not only was he the most generous boss she'd ever had, but the most attractive too. If she wasn't so in love with her husband she could have fallen for Steel in a big way, she thought—for possibly the thousandth time. Perhaps she was in love with him a little, but he'd always been so businesslike and correct in his dealings with her it had been easy to conceal it.

Outside, the warm June air carried city dust and fumes in its embrace, but once in his black Aston Martin Steel relaxed a little. He liked driving and the car was a dream, the air conditioning and state-of-the-art luxury making the experience pleasurable even in the worst London snarl-ups. He drove automatically, his mind on Annie. She and Jeff had been trying for this baby for a long time; ever since they'd married, in fact, three years previously. At twenty-six, Annie was twelve years younger than him and he had virtually brought her up when their parents had been killed in a car accident when Annie was six years old. He'd been about to go away to university but he'd got a job instead, and this income, added to his half of the nest egg which his parents had been accumulating in the bank, had meant he could continue to pay the rent on the three-bedroomed house that had been home. Annie had lost their parents, he hadn't wanted her to lose the familiarity and security of the home she'd lived in all her life. Annie's half of the estate had been in trust until she was eighteen and had been a nice little inheritance for her.

They had managed. His mind wandered to the years of Annie's childhood. Their paternal grandparents had already died, but his mother's mother and father had stepped into the breach and looked after Annie every day after school until he collected her from them. Neighbours and friends had also been kind. And now Annie was a beautiful, well-adjusted young woman, and he was in a good place. Independent, autonomous, answerable to no one and no one relying on him.

Not that he'd resented caring for Annie. His mind immediately dealt with the issue as though someone had put the idea to him. He'd done it because he wanted to. Pure and simple. But the long years until she had met Jeff when she'd been twenty-one had taught him something. He didn't want to be responsible for another human being again. He wanted a life free of emotional liability and obligation. A life where he could take off at the drop of a hat. No involved arrangements. No explanations. No...*accountability*. He'd done his time with all that—from the age of eighteen until he was thirty-three. Fifteen years. And now he relished his freedom, fed on it.

He'd had girlfriends from the age of puberty: a few long term, most ships that passed after a couple of months, due—he had to admit—to his determination to continue in the single state once his parents had died. Now he dated sophisticated, career-obsessed women:

females who were as wary of commitment and for ever as he was. It worked—mostly. The last lady in his life, an intelligent, fiercely independent—or so he'd thought—lawyer, had suddenly decided she wanted to move in with him.

Barbara flashed on the screen of his mind: sultry, voluptuous—the sort of attorney who could have the opposition admitting anything with one look from her feline eyes. Their parting had been less than harmonious. That had been a couple of weeks ago, and although he missed her enticing and provocative body in his bed he had no doubts he'd done the right thing in ending their relationship.

His hand touched the back of his neck briefly as he recalled the resounding slap she'd delivered. It had all but cracked the bones in his neck as his head had jerked back with the force of it, and this from the woman who had insisted *forever* was a dirty word when they'd first got together.

Women... His firm, sensual mouth tightened for a moment. They were another species. Not that he'd given up on them; what red-blooded man would? And nine times out of ten it worked out fine. When the end of the relationship came there were no tears, no scenes, no recriminations. He was still friends with the majority of his exes; that had to say something.

It wasn't as if he was ever less than completely honest. He made it a rule to be clear about his intentions from the first date. No promises, no roses round the door, just two healthy human beings sharing their lives and beds for a while. Straightforward and simple. Just the way he liked it.

The traffic was a nightmare. It took him nearly an hour to reach the hospital. When he pulled into the car park he found his heart was thudding with anxiety and his stomach was turning over with fear of what he might find inside. It was further proof—if he'd needed any— that he didn't want anyone else other than Annie to have a piece of his heart.

Steel straightened his shoulders, reached for the enormous bouquet of yellow roses and white freesias he'd picked up en route and got out of the car.

Her hands were shaking, not something that was likely to inspire confidence in a prospective employer. And from what she knew of Steel Landry he would expect a cool, composed and completely professional approach.

Toni willed the tremors to cease as she tried breathing slowly and deeply. She'd read somewhere that worked for nerves.

It didn't. All it did do was to make her feel slightly light-headed and now she was ten times more panic-stricken. What if she fainted at Steel Landry's feet?

Rising from the edge of the sofa she was perched on, Toni walked across to the large bay window and stared down into the busy London street three stories below. The excellent double glazing meant traffic noise was reduced to a mere whisper, and although the pavements were crowded no sound from the people below penetrated her luxurious surroundings. And they *were* luxurious...

Turning, she surveyed the fabulous room Steel Landry's 'daily'—as the small bustling woman who had answered the door had described herself—had shown her into when she had arrived at the impressive South Kensington flat ten minutes ago. The cream and dove-grey sitting room was all soft leather sofas, glass tables and light maple wood. Several bowls of fresh flowers scented the air and a beautiful cream marble fireplace with floor-to-ceiling glass bookshelves in the alcoves either side provided the focus of the room.

Luxurious, stunning and clearly meant to impress any visitors, but a little...cold for her liking, Toni decided. It was as though the person living here had no intention of giving anything of himself away. Which would fit the little she knew of Steel Landry to a T.

She didn't have time to reflect further. The door opened and a tall, dark-haired man strode into the room. 'Sorry to have kept you waiting; an urgent call I had to take which couldn't wait. Steel Landry, and you must be Toni George? Sit down, won't you? Maggie's bringing us coffee in a moment or two,' he added, shaking her hand.

Toni was glad to sink down on one of the sofas. James had described Steel as a handsome so-and-so, and he hadn't been wrong. The dark, rugged good looks were certainly attractive but it was his piercing silver-blue eyes that had thrown her. His lashes were thick and black and framed the metallic orbs dramatically, emphasising the silvery hue to his blue eyes perfectly. Many a model would have paid a fortune to have eyes like his, she thought inconsequentially. It didn't seem fair nature had wasted them on a man.

Before she could voice the polite 'It's nice to meet you' social opening appropriate for such occasions, he further threw her when he said, 'May I take your coat?'

This necessitated her standing up again and as he helped her off with the coat she caught a faint whiff of his aftershave, a subtle blend that held warm, woody notes and a hint of citrus fruits. She shivered involuntarily, glad he had turned away to lay her coat over the back of one of the sofas so he didn't notice. Toni was tall at five feet ten, but he had towered over her by another six or seven inches and she had found it disconcerting. She found *him* disconcerting.

Nevertheless, by the time he had sat down opposite her she was outwardly composed, her voice calm and smooth when she said, 'Thank you for seeing me today, Mr Landry. I know how busy you are. I hope your sister is feeling better.'

He frowned. It clearly hadn't been the best thing to say.

'She's pregnant and things aren't going too well,' he said briefly, the tone of his voice ending further comment.

Toni knew her cheeks had turned pink but there was nothing she could do about it. Gamely, she struggled on. 'I've brought my portfolio for you to look at with a list of past clients who would be only too pleased to give me a reference should you require it. I—'

The cutting motion of his hand stopped her in mid-flow. Leaning forward, he fixed her with his eyes. 'I've already made my own enquiries before I agreed to this interview. James is the best architect I know but he'd be the first to admit he's no interior designer. When he mentioned you in passing for this job he said very little beyond you were a damn good designer and you'd worked for his practice for six years before leaving to start a family just over four years ago. Is that correct?'

'I— Yes. Yes, that's correct.'

'And now you want to get back into the workplace and take up your career?'

'Yes.' Toni felt as though she were a prisoner being interrogated. On the rack.

'Why?' Steel Landry asked coolly.

'I beg your pardon?'

'Why do you want to return to work? Was it always part of the plan after a specific amount of time or are you bored or are there financial implications? And are you sure you've done having babies?'

She couldn't believe this. It wasn't so much what he said as the way he said it, but that last bit about having babies had been downright aggressive. Or it felt like that anyway.

Toni's deep brown eyes took on the consistency of polished onyx. Her small chin rose sharply. 'Quite sure, Mr Landry,' she said crisply. 'And my reasons for resuming my career are my own business.'

'Wrong.' The silver gaze held hers and his voice was lazy and without heat. 'I'm sure James explained I'm looking to diversify from what has hitherto been a property business encapsulating office blocks, shops, warehouses, that type of thing? This latest venture is a conversion of an old factory into several apartments for the very rich, and I mean *very* rich. They'll expect nothing less than the best from the smallest, most functional item in their home to the biggest. Space-age technology but without losing the cosy feel-good factor. I could have employed any number of excellent interior designers but a chance conversation with James raised your name. This first project is merely a stepping stone. I want the right folk on side from the beginning, people who are in it for the long haul.'

Toni nodded. What James had *actually* said was that Steel Landry got bored easily, and his business, which had begun with the purchase of the odd property or two, had swiftly grown into a vast network of prime real estate that had made him too successful. She'd laughed, asking how anyone could be too successful, and he'd told her Steel was a restless spirit, the sort of man who wasn't happy unless he was wrestling with a challenge. Consequently, James had said, the Midas touch Steel had was both a blessing and a curse.

'The person I employ is likely to have their own team in a couple of years with the accompanying responsibility. For that reason I think I have every right to question your motives and satisfy myself this return to the workplace is not on a whim.'

Acknowledging this was perfectly reasonable, Toni nodded again. 'I can assure you this is no whim, Mr Landry,' she said, willing her voice not to tremble. 'My return to work is born out of necessity financially.'

The metallic eyes narrowed. 'And your husband would not object to your having a demanding career? And what about childcare?'

'He— I—' Oh, for goodness' sake pull yourself together, Toni told herself desperately. She had expected these sort of questions, hadn't she?

Yes, a separate part of her mind answered. But not someone like Steel Landry asking them. And this was the first time she had laid the searingly painful events of the last months bare to a stranger. Nevertheless, she couldn't let emotion get in the way.

Taking a deep breath, she composed herself. 'My husband died unexpectedly leaving huge debts,' she said flatly, 'and childcare is not an issue. We—my children and I—are staying with my parents for the time being. My mother is available for them.'

A tap at the door preceded the daily appearing with a tray of coffee and cake. Bustling over to them, she laid the tray on a low coffee table as she chirruped, 'I've made you one of my fruit cakes, Mr Landry. Joy said you hadn't eaten your lunch when she called earlier and dinner won't be ready till eight.'

Steel sat back in his chair and the smile he gave the little woman made Toni's heart jolt. Serious, he was drop-dead gorgeous, but when he smiled... Dynamite. It increased the smouldering sex appeal about a thousand per cent.

'Thanks, Maggie,' he said lazily, 'although I doubt I'm in danger of wasting away.'

'Be that as it may, it doesn't do to skip meals.' Maggie's demeanour was one of motherly reproof; Toni had the feeling the daily and her formidable employer got on very well. This was borne out when the little woman poured them both a cup of coffee and cut Steel a massive slice of cake, clucking her tongue at Toni when she refused a piece. 'You young girls these days.' She shook her grey head. 'Don't eat enough to keep a sparrow alive. How about just a morsel to have with your coffee, eh?'

Helplessly, Toni agreed. It was simpler.

Satisfied, the daily gave them both a beaming smile and bustled out of the room, her permed curls bobbing.

Toni looked down at the plate on her lap and then raised her eyes to find Steel Landry's gaze on her face. 'Are you always persuaded so easily?' he murmured, before adding, 'You said children. How many do you have?'

She knew her face was burning with colour when she reached into her briefcase and brought out the CV she hadn't had time to send before the interview. James had only called her the night before to say he'd mentioned her name to Steel Landry and he'd agreed to see her the next evening after checking out some of her previous work. She'd grabbed the opportunity with both hands.

'M-my personal details are included,' she mumbled as she held the plastic folder out to him.

He didn't take it. 'I prefer to hear it from you.'

Great. 'I have twin girls.'

'How old are they?'

'Nearly four.' She placed the folder on the coffee table.

She wasn't aware how her voice had softened at the thought of Amelia and Daisy, but the silver eyes watching her so intently sharpened. 'And you'd be happy to work evenings and weekends when necessary?' he asked quietly. 'This is no nine-to-five job.'

Another fair question and one that could lose her any chance of getting the job if she answered honestly. 'Not happy, no,' she said stiffly. 'But I know they'd be well cared for and I have to work. It's as simple as that.'

He considered her over the rim of his coffee cup. 'Another personal question. You said huge debts. That means what exactly? Ballpark figure if you don't mind.'

This was worse than she'd imagined. Knowing her hands were shaking, Toni put down the coffee cup and gripped them together in her lap. 'Eighty thousand pounds,' she said flatly.

She raised her head and looked at him. His face was impassive. No doubt eighty thousand was pocket change to him, but to her it was a small fortune. She swallowed hard. He might as well know it all. 'My husband had taken loans out all over the place,' she said tightly. 'Most of them were wiped out with his death but he'd borrowed from friends and family too, even work colleagues. He told so many stories…' She gulped, determined to get through without breaking down. She'd done enough crying lately to last a lifetime and employers didn't like hysterical women.

'What did he want the money for?'

'Gambling.' One word, but as stark and ugly as any profanity as far as Toni was concerned, and her tone reflected this.

'And you didn't know?'

He sounded faintly incredulous. Toni didn't blame him. She found it unbelievable herself. She'd lived with Richard for over four years and she hadn't known him at all, apparently.

It had been a textbook whirlwind marriage. They had met at the wedding of one of Toni's old university friends, and had been wed themselves within three months. He had been charming and carefree and funny and she'd fallen for him like a ton of bricks. By the time doubts had set in she'd found she'd become pregnant with the twins on honeymoon. Fait accompli.

'No, I didn't know.' Her eyes were deep pools of pain. 'But I intend to pay back every penny he borrowed.'

'How many people does that involve?'

She felt nauseous remembering. 'A lot,' she said bleakly.

'And none of them would wipe the slate clean considering you knew nothing about your husband's addiction?'

'I wouldn't let them.' Her chin had a proud tilt to it now. 'However long it takes, they'll get their money.'

He surveyed her for a long moment without speaking and then drank the rest of his coffee. It was only when he replaced the cup on the saucer that he said softly, 'Even at the cost of your children's welfare.'

For a moment she wondered if she'd heard right.

Then, stung beyond measure, she glared at him as she got to her feet. 'My children will always come first with me. *Always*. But that doesn't mean I can't do what's right.'

'You're sure this isn't your pride having a field day?'

Hateful man. 'Richard stole from our friends and family,' she bit out angrily. 'Oh, he might have dressed it up differently, but that's what he did. He lied and cheated and would probably be doing the same now if he hadn't had a massive heart attack when out jogging one evening. One old aunt lent him her life savings. She's barely got enough now to feed herself and her cats.'

'They can't all be elderly and destitute,' Steel commented mildly, seemingly untouched by her anger.

'No, but they all trusted my husband and were cruelly let down. Betrayed through no fault of their own.'

'As you were.'

Toni blinked. She had been set to walk out a second ago, now she didn't know what to do. The way he'd said the last words had brought the traitorous tears close to the surface again.

'Sit down and finish your coffee and cake,' he said very softly, and when, after a second's hesitation, she complied he continued to observe her.

Behind the cool, unruffled exterior Steel's mind was racing. For once he found himself at something of a loss and he didn't like that. When he had first walked into the room and seen the young woman in the pistachio-green coat standing by the window his male antenna had responded with appreciation to the womanly shape topped by a mass of dark brown hair.

Toni George was attractive, very attractive. Not beautiful, he qualified, although many a model would have killed for her cheekbones, but she had something, something indefinable. When he had relieved her of her coat he'd caught the scent of her perfume and it had caused his loins to tighten. Ridiculous, but he'd found himself wishing she wasn't a married woman...

*Be careful what you wish for because it might just come true.* Who'd said that? Whoever, they were dead right, he thought with dark amusement, because any involvement with a widow with two young children—a definitely damaged and troubled widow at that—spelt nothing but disaster.

Becoming aware where his thoughts had led, he mentally shook his head. What the hell was he playing at? This young woman had come to see him about a job, that was all, and with what she'd been through in the last months she'd no more be looking for anything of a romantic nature than a trip to the moon. And someone in her position—no matter how attractive they were— could never feature on his agenda. She was as different from the kind of woman he dated as chalk from cheese.

Steel reached for the folder on the table between them, opening it and taking out the neat pages it contained. Swiftly he scanned the facts and figures within. Personal details were at a minimum.

Her velvet-brown eyes were waiting for him when he looked up and he was aware she was jumpy. It had no relevance to what he'd just been reading but, because he wanted to know, he said, 'How long have you been widowed?'

She shifted slightly in the seat. 'Nearly four months.'

Four months of hell, if the look on her face was anything to go by. To his amazement, he heard himself say,

'Were you happy with him? Before he died and you discovered the debts?'

She stiffened and he waited for her to tell him to mind his own business. He wouldn't have blamed her.

Instead, after a long ten seconds had ticked by, she lowered her head so the sleek thick curtain of shoulder-length hair swung to conceal her expression. 'No, I wasn't happy.'

There was a red light burning bright and hot in his mind. Obeying it, he turned his concentration to her CV, talking through a couple of points with her. Then he looked at her portfolio. It was impressive, as he'd expected it to be; he wouldn't have wasted his time granting her an interview otherwise.

She was confident and enthusiastic when discussing her work, metamorphosing into a different person in front of his fascinated gaze. This is what she would have been like when she met that louse she married, Steel thought with a bolt of quite unreasonably vicious hatred for the dead man. Energised, self-assured, daunt-less. And he'd been wrong earlier. She *was* beautiful. Enchantingly so.

It was close to half-past six when he asked her if she'd like to see the plans and photographs of the project thus far. When, nearly an hour later, he noticed her glance surreptitiously at her watch he couldn't believe how the time had flown. 'I'm sorry, do you need to be somewhere?' he said as her colour flared, indicating she was aware he'd caught her checking the time.

'No, no, of course not.' Toni knew she should have left it at that in view of the fact she'd previously assured him the twins wouldn't be an issue regarding her work-ing late. Instead she found herself continuing, 'It's just that it's the girls' bedtime and I always ring them if I'm not there to tuck them in.'

Steel straightened. He didn't want to think of her as a mother, which in itself indicated a mental step backwards away from this dark-haired woman with the huge eyes and delicious body was called for. He smiled thinly. 'Go ahead.' He gestured at the telephone on a glass table next to an enormous bowl of hothouse blooms. 'I need to call the hospital again anyway.'

'I've got my mobile...'

She was fumbling in one of the huge handbags women seem to favour these days and he was suddenly intensely irritated without knowing why. 'No need. I'll use the other line in my study,' he said coolly, walking to the door as he spoke and shutting it firmly behind him once he was in the hall. He stood there for a moment, collecting his thoughts.

What was the matter with him, for crying out loud? He breathed deeply, his nostrils flaring. So she was phoning her kids. So what? He knew she wasn't first and foremost a career-motivated Barbara with her own flat and sports car and intrinsically selfish life that meant she could do what she wanted, when she wanted and how she wanted. And with whom. He hadn't even known she existed until a day or two ago. She meant nothing to him. Nothing beyond a potential employee, that was. If he should choose to give her the job.

He walked into his study and reached for the telephone on the massive curving desk in front of the window. It was only then he acknowledged there was no *if* about it. She'd had the job from the minute he'd laid eyes on her.

He shook his head at himself. Steady, boy, steady, he cautioned silently. Big step backwards here. He didn't do impulsive. Every decision he made was logical and thought out, even ruthless at times. It was how he had created a thriving little empire in just under twenty years. Sentiment and emotion were all very well but they had no place in business.

He was frowning as he rang Jeff's mobile, but after talking to his brother-in-law for a couple of minutes and finding out Annie was no worse his expression cleared.

Toni George would be just another employee. Anything else was not acceptable. Decision made, he stood up, flexed his broad shoulders and left the room.

# CHAPTER TWO

TONI'S MOTHER ANSWERED the telephone. Toni could hear shrieks of laughter and high squeals in the background as she said, 'Mother? It's me. I'm not going to be back for a while yet—the interview still hasn't finished. I was ringing to say goodnight to the girls. Are they ready for bed?' Their bedtime was seven-thirty but if she wasn't around to enforce it, it could be any time, which invariably meant two tetchy little girls the next day. Not good for them or anyone around them!

'Oh, yes, love. They've had their bath and they're in their pyjamas,' Vivienne Otley said fondly.

Hating to be critical, but knowing how long it took the twins to calm down once they got excited, Toni said carefully, 'I thought we'd agreed seven was the deadline for reading stories in bed so they can wind down?'

'Well, you know what your father's like with them. He's the big bad wolf and they're the little pigs. I'm a little pig too.'

Toni stifled a sigh. She adored her parents and would be eternally grateful for the way they'd immediately opened up their home and hearts to her and the twins when the full horror of the mountain of debts came to light, but she was fighting a losing battle against the girls being spoilt rotten.

Having tried unsuccessfully for a child for years, her parents had long since resigned themselves to being childless when she'd made her appearance on her mother's forty-second birthday thirty years ago. Her mother's favourite story was that for the first six months of pregnancy Toni had been dismissed as the onset of the menopause. It had only been when she gave a hefty kick one day that her mother had realised the flutters and discomfort she'd put down to her age and flatulence were, in fact, a baby. A nine-pound baby as it turned out.

Toni had always known she was her parents' sun, moon and stars, but in spite of their joy in their beloved daughter they had never spoiled her. Just the contrary in fact. But with the twins... Suppressing another sigh, she said meaningfully, 'Put them on the line, would you, and I'll make it clear they're straight to bed. They've got that nursery trip tomorrow to the safari park and they're going to be exhausted if they're up late.'

Amelia came on the phone first, as Toni had expected. The older twin by minutes, Amelia led and Daisy followed. ''Lo, Mummy,' Amelia said brightly. 'Grandad's pretending to be the wolf and he's put those big teeth in we got in a cracker at Christmas. He's nearly swallowed them once.' Lowering her voice, she whispered, 'We're acting scared but we aren't really.'

Toni had to smile. 'Hallo, honeybee,' she said softly. 'I'm not going to be able to get home to put you to bed so I'm sending a big kiss and hug down the phone, OK? And I want you to promise you'll go straight to bed now and Grandma will read you one story. You've got your trip tomorrow, haven't you? And you don't want to miss anything because you're too tired.'

It worked. 'All right, Mummy,' Amelia said at once,

handing the phone to her sister before Toni could say goodbye.

''Lo, Mummy,' Daisy lisped, her voice softer and more babyish than Amelia's. 'When are you coming home?'

'Soon, darling, but Grandma's going to read your story tonight and tuck you in because Mummy's trying to get that job I told you and Amelia about. Remember? Be a good girl for Grandma, won't you? Go straight to sleep, promise me?'

'Yesp.' A tiny pause. 'I lub you, Mummy.'

'I love you, sweetpea.' Swallowing the lump in her throat, she added, 'I'll come and kiss you when I get home, but I want you to go straight to sleep after your story.'

Her mother came on the line. 'She's nodding to whatever you just said, bless her. And I'm sorry, love. I forgot about that nursery trip. It's gone clean out of my mind.'

Toni felt instantly guilty. Why should her parents *have* to remember about things like nursery trips at their age? They were in their early seventies; they should be enjoying the grandchildren visiting every so often for a few hours, not being with them full time. Richard hadn't paid the rent on the flat they'd been living in for a while before he'd died, but even if they'd been up to date there was no way they could have continued to live there on what she could earn. A basic bedsit would be all she could afford and it would mean she wouldn't be able to save anything towards paying off the mountain of debt Richard had left. Her parents continued to insist they loved having her and the grandchildren and wouldn't hear of her moving out, but their small two-bedroomed terrace was bursting at the seams with the children's paraphernalia. She slept on a sofa bed in the sitting room at night and she knew her parents' calm, orderly life had been turned upside down. But what was the alternative?

Wearily she brushed a strand of dark brown hair laced with copper behind her ear. She was tired. Mentally and emotionally worn out, and she couldn't think beyond this present moment or she'd lose any faint hope she had of landing this job. James had assured her Steel would pay well, exceptionally well if he thought she was the right person for the job. Steel's employees rarely left the firm, he'd said drily, in spite of his reputation of being an exacting employer. An excellent salary and a generous package of benefits bought loyalty.

When Steel returned to the room she was sitting primly on the sofa, her manner one of cool compo-sure. This lasted all of one moment due to him saying smoothly, 'Maggie assures me there is more than enough dinner for two, Mrs George, and, as we haven't finished the interview yet and I'm hungry, it seems sensible to kill two birds with one stone. Unless you have any objection, of course?'

Plenty, but she couldn't very well say so. For a second or two she sat there dry-mouthed, his impossibly light eyes seeming to pin her to the spot. It took some effort to pull herself together but her voice was gratifyingly steady when she said, 'That's very kind of you, Mr Landry. Thank you.'

'Maggie will call us when the meal's ready but in the meantime can I offer you a drink?' He was walking across to the beautifully made glass cocktail cabinet in a corner or the room as he spoke. 'I usually have a cocktail about this time of night if I'm not driving, but there's red, white or rosé wine, along with various spirits and mixers, sherry, martini...'

'A cocktail would be lovely.' She was glad now she'd eaten the slice of cake Maggie had pressed on her. The day had been hectic and after she had dropped the twins off at their nursery she'd rushed from pillar to post and skipped lunch. Without the cake any alcohol would have gone straight to her head, but she felt Steel Landry would expect a sophisticated career woman to have a pre-dinner aperitif.

She watched as he prepared the cocktails, and as he carried two glasses back to where she was sitting she took one with a smile of thanks. 'What is it?'

'A Moscow Mule.'

He smiled, and her heart did a pancake flip. She took a tiny sip and the zingy concoction exploded on her taste buds and then left a warm glow where it travelled.

'Despite its name it was invented in a Sunset Strip bar in 1940s Hollywood,' Steel said lazily, sitting down opposite her once more and loosening his tie as he undid the top two buttons of his shirt.

It made concentrating on what he was saying hard, doubly so as he crossed one leg over the other knee and settled back comfortably. It was crazy, ridiculous, but every nerve in her body was registering his smallest action and she didn't know why. Perhaps it was because he was the most aggressively masculine man she'd ever met, and his voice—deep, smoky, compelling—added to the dark sexual appeal.

Summoning her thought process, Toni said weakly, 'What's in it? It tastes pretty powerful.'

He nodded his agreement. 'Russian wheat vodka, lime juice and ginger beer. Apparently a spirits distributor was having trouble getting the Americans to buy his Russian vodka so he thought up a new drink with a barman who made his own, equally poorly selling, ginger beer. Enterprising, especially as it lives up to their marketing of having a kick like a mule.'

And Steel Landry was a man who would appreciate enterprise and initiative, she thought. Did he realise how intimidating he was? Probably. It was a tool that would serve him well in the cut-throat world of business. Wishing her neatly tailored, pencil-slim skirt were a couple of inches longer—although its knee-length had never bothered her before—she covertly tugged at it and readjusted her position before taking another sip of the cocktail.

'Kids OK?' he asked softly.

Startled, she met his gaze. 'Yes, they're fine.'

'Then could you try to relax a little?'

'I beg your pardon?' Painfully aware she'd turned an unflattering shade of crimson, Toni didn't know where to put herself. 'I am perfectly relaxed, thank you.'

'You, Mrs George, are like a cat on a hot tin roof,' he drawled slowly, 'or maybe little Miss Riding Hood in front of the big bad wolf would be a better analogy. Whatever, I'm not going to try to seduce you over drinks and dinner.'

'I never thought for a moment you were,' she said hotly, such transparent honesty in her voice he couldn't fail to believe her.

His eyes narrowed. 'Then why so tense?'

She shrugged. How could she say she was desperate for the job? That it would make all the difference in the world to her if he paid half as well as James had intimated he might? She had enjoyed her time working for James's practice; preparing the sketches and ideas for quotation and then, if the practice won the contract, putting together more detailed specifications and working drawings and getting approval for them. Once she'd put out the contract for the actual work—the decorating, furniture, coverings, etc.—to tender, she had been responsible for supervising it and seeing schedules were kept and problems solved. It had been tough sometimes when things went wrong but she'd been good at it and she *knew* she could handle anything Steel Landry might ask of her. The alternative was trying to pick up some freelance work or another job, both of which were in short supply to someone who'd been out of the running for the last four years.

She didn't regret her time at home with the twins. Richard had had a very good job as a sales executive for a large pharmaceutical company and they should have been able to manage perfectly well until the twins started school and she went into the workplace again. She had been very careful to shop wisely and make a penny stretch to two, making the most of two-for-one offers and learning how to cook the cheaper cuts of meat until they were as tender as anything offered at the best restaurants. Most of the girls' clothes she'd made herself, copying the latest designer fashions with such success she'd earnt a little extra for the family finances when friends had asked her to do the same for them. She hadn't realised at the time that her efforts were pointless and that Richard's double life was about to blow their family apart. She'd been so gullible and stupid.

'Mrs George?'

The deep, slightly husky voice brought her out of the darkness. She blinked. He wanted an answer to his question. Following on from her thoughts, she said hesitantly, 'I—I suppose I'm out of practice regarding interviews and selling myself.'

Even if she hadn't realised instantly the last words weren't the best she could have chosen, the way the carved lips twitched slightly would have told her, but his voice was soothing when he murmured, 'Not at all. You've done an excellent job.'

Her soft brown eyes sharpened. She didn't know how to take that. She didn't know how to take *him*. When James had rung her she'd done a little research of her own on the powerhouse that was Steel Landry. She'd wished she hadn't afterwards; it had made her more nervous. A human dynamo. Hard but fair. Relentless and unmovable when he wanted something. Severely lacking in the milk of human kindness. Admittedly that last had been from a disgruntled ex-employee who hadn't been up to the position for which he had been employed, but nevertheless it had been unsettling.

'Drink your cocktail, Mrs George,' he said smoothly, 'and stop worrying. You've got the job if you want it, OK?'

'I have?' Her eyes opened wide with startled pleasure. 'Thank you. Thank you so much, Mr Landry.'

'You accept?' he asked, as though there had ever been a chance she might refuse. 'Good. In that case we can do away with the Mr Landry and Mrs George. The name's Steel.'

'But—' She stopped, not knowing how to continue.

'What?'

'You—you're my boss,' she stammered stupidly.

The crystal eyes crinkled. 'Did you call James by his surname?' he asked mildly, finishing his cocktail.

'No, but—' She paused. 'That—that's different.'

'Why? He was your boss, wasn't he?'

Yes, but James hadn't been the head of a small empire worth umpteen millions, and neither had he been drop-dead gorgeous. 'Things were quite informal at James's practice,' she said weakly.

He nodded. 'And my employees who work closely with me enjoy that same privilege; my secretary, for example, and my financial director to name but two. This is a new project and I'll want to be involved at every stage so you'll be working *particularly* hand in glove with me. Steel and Toni will do just fine.'

Toni was kicking herself for objecting. Whatever must he be thinking? He'd just surprised her, that was all. Pulling herself together, she said quickly, 'Of course. Thank you. Thank you so much. I won't let you down, I promise.'

'Believe me, Toni, if I had any doubt about that I wouldn't be offering you the job.'

She did believe him, and strangely his belief in her was both uplifting and scary at the same time. Uplifting because her self-confidence had taken the mother and father of a knock over the last months, scary because the pressure to show him he'd been right to give her the job had suddenly increased a hundredfold just with hearing him say her name. Silly. Irrational. Emotions a man like Steel Landry would despise.

She raised her chin in a businesslike manner and assumed a look she prayed was professional. 'When would you like me to start?'

'We'll discuss the details over dinner, including salary,' he said gently.

The reminder that she hadn't even asked the basics before accepting the position brought telltale colour to her cheeks again, but this time she didn't falter. She even managed to inject a suggestion of sophisticated amuse-ment into her tone when she said, 'I've always adhered to the idea you get what you are prepared to pay for in this world.'

'Is that so?' he said silkily, his eyes intent on her flushed face. 'Then I hope your salary buys everything I need from you, Toni…'

## CHAPTER THREE

TONI WAS ETERNALLY grateful that Maggie chose to knock on the door and announce dinner was ready the moment after Steel had spoken. She wasn't sure if he'd put a different connotation to her words than that which she'd intended—it could just be her fevered imagination—but as he rose and ushered her out of the sitting room with a cool hand in the small of her back she knew her cheeks were burning afresh.

She had expected to eat in a formal dining room, so when he led the way out onto a spectacular roof terrace she caught her breath in surprise. The terrace was laid out as a dining room and living space with stylish furniture; olive, eucalyptus and silver birch trees in huge white pots surrounding the perimeter all underplanted with a mix of grasses, lavender, iris, allium and other plants creating a vista reminiscent of woodland and Mediterranean scenes. The glass balustrade kept the space serene and light-filled as well as enabling the view to be appreciated, a view that seemed to take in the whole of Kensington. The dining table had been made from a slab of white Carrara marble and was a thing of beauty in itself, and the exterior sofas and easy chairs on the other side of the terrace to the dining suite were grouped round a marble coffee table with a built-in fireplace.

Toni stood, completely stunned, her artistic antenna quivering as her mind and senses struggled to take in what she was seeing. 'This is beautiful.' She breathed out the words slowly. 'Absolutely beautiful. Who designed it?'

His smile had a self-mocking edge. 'I did.'

'You?'

Her amazement wasn't exactly complimentary but fortunately he seemed more amused than offended. 'I can appreciate beauty as much as the next man,' he murmured as he pulled out one of the dining chairs for her to sit down, 'in spite of being that most crass of creatures, a property developer.'

'But if you can do this why wouldn't you want to plan and carry out your own ideas on this new venture?' she asked, stroking the fine marble under her fingers. The table was set for two with silver cutlery and crystal galore, a bowl of white lilies scenting the warm evening air.

He didn't answer immediately, walking round to the other side of the table and reaching for the wine in the ice bucket. 'I thought champagne was in order as this is a celebration.' He passed her a glass full of the sparkling liquid and poured one for himself, raising it as he said, 'To a long and happy working relationship.'

She could second that. 'Thank you.' She didn't actually like champagne, she'd always found it too much on the dry side for her taste buds, but as she took a sip of the effervescent bubbles she realised there was champagne and champagne, and this one was like nothing she'd tasted before. Honey, strawberries, summer days and lazy nights, they were all there in the delicious and no doubt wildly expensive wine.

'And in answer to your question regarding why I need you, Toni,' he went on softly, 'this terrace is a one-off as far as I'm concerned. I knew what *I* wanted so it was easy, even though it took me two months of intensive planning and the odd sleepless night when work commenced, but I wouldn't want to think up ideas for someone else, time after time.'

The boredom factor again, she thought intuitively. He was indeed a restless spirit. What had made him that way? Bringing her thoughts back into line, she glanced round her surroundings again as she said, 'I can see this must have cost you a great deal of money. You said you want the best for these new apartments; do you mean going this far if necessary?'

'Absolutely.'

Now they were sitting down the trees and foliage provided a privacy that was curiously intimate; a small green world up in the sky with only the odd London bird to spy on the occupants below. Toni was vitally aware of this as he leant forward slightly, speaking with an intensity she was almost sure he was unaware of when he went on, 'It's important this first phase has an impact, and money is no object—my buyers will be able to afford it. Each apartment needs to be different and, as you've already seen from the plans, this was borne in mind from the word go. But they all have to be outstanding. I want you to play around with designs and ideas, think laterally, enjoy yourself.'

He seemed to check himself as though exerting some sort of personal rein, the silver-blue eyes hiding their expression. They reminded her of shells found on a windswept beach and washed clean by the constant tides to reveal the cool mother-of-pearl beneath. She had never seen eyes like them in a human face before.

He didn't like showing emotion, she thought suddenly. Even about his business. Did emotion translate as weakness in that hard, cold male mind? Without considering her words, she asked what she'd been wanting to ask since he'd returned after the phone call. 'How's your sister?'

After a brief pause he took a swallow of champagne before saying, 'Too soon to really be sure, but better, Jeff, her husband, seemed to think. Things are stabilizing, settling down. She has to have complete bedrest for the foreseeable future, though, which won't suit Annie. She can't keep still for two minutes.'

There was deep affection in his voice and he seemed more relaxed about talking about his sister than he had earlier. Carefully, she said, 'How many months pregnant is she?'

He thought for a moment. 'I'm not sure,' he admitted ruefully. 'That doesn't say much for the prospective uncle, does it? Two months, three months, something like that. Nothing to be seen yet anyway.'

'I had a friend who was in a similar condition a couple of years ago. With complete rest the pregnancy went on until the thirty-third week and although Jack was premature he's the brightest toddler I've ever come across. Tell your sister to endure what needs to be endured and not take any chances.'

Steel nodded. He liked the fact she hadn't offered the normal platitudes of 'I'm sure she's going to be all right,' and 'They can do such marvelous things these days.' In fact he liked Toni George altogether. He let his eyes wander over her face, lingering for a moment on the soft full curve of her lips. He wondered what it would feel like to have that mouth open beneath his, to penetrate the sweet interior.

The thought was simple but it sent a bolt of desire sizzling through his body and he turned as hard as a rock. Shocked at how such an innocent fantasy could have such an immediate effect, he moved his gaze to the skyline. He was, by virtue of his intelligence and instinct, a very rational man, perhaps even cynical, he admitted silently. He conducted his love life in the same controlled way he ran the rest of his life and boyish, passionate irrationalism had had no place in his dealings with the opposite sex for two decades or more. He had a rigid list of personal codes and values and one rule was inexorable. No mixing business and pleasure.

Over the years he had watched too many people, some of them good friends, become entangled in messy relationships with work colleagues and the fallout when the affair ended was invariably embarrassing at best and painful at worst. It was rare one person wasn't left feeling bruised and hurt and the tension and difficulties that could arise made work life uncomfortable. Knowing this, why had he asked this woman to have dinner with him tonight? He could easily have wrapped up the interview in five minutes. It was illogical, a trait he prided himself he'd escaped. He'd gone against everything he'd told himself earlier.

Irritated with himself, he became aware she was looking at him with some concern and realised he was frowning again.

'I'm sorry,' she said quickly, her words tumbling over themselves. 'I shouldn't have presumed to tell your sister what to do. It's nothing to do with me.'

Far from pacifying him, her words made him more nettled, but he couldn't have said why. Forcing a smile, he told himself he was being ridiculous. 'Not at all; it's kind of you to be concerned,' he said coolly, his tone negating the words. 'Now back to business. How soon could you start?'

'Straight away,' she said eagerly. 'Whenever you like.'

'Monday morning? That will give you the rest of the week to put arrangements in place regarding any domestic arrangements.'

Toni found she resented her precious girls being written off as 'domestic arrangements'. Purposely, she said, 'Thank you, that would be welcome, although very little will change at home. As I mentioned before, my parents are on hand to take care of Amelia and Daisy. What—what would be my normal working hours?'

Amelia and Daisy. Were they two little miniatures of her or did they look like their swine of a father? Repressing the notion to ask her if she had a photograph of the children, he said quietly, 'It's the sort of position where "normal" working hours won't apply some of the time, as I'm sure you'll appreciate having seen jobs for James's practice through from beginning to end. However, I do expect my staff to put in a good day's work for a good day's pay, but as long as you do that the hours can be flexible within reason. I have other employees with children on the payroll and, depending on nursery or school hours and the various panics and situations which occur in family life, they juggle their hours accordingly.'

Steel could tell from the widening of the velvet brown eyes that she hadn't expected him to be so reasonable. He was glad he'd been able to surprise her, but it rankled she obviously thought him something of a tyrant. Keeping the annoyance he was feeling out of his voice, he went on, 'There will be times when you will be able to work from home if necessary and other periods when it will be essential you are in the office or visiting the site. At those times I expect my business to take precedence over anything else, barring life-or-death family issues, of course.'

'Of course.' She nodded briskly.

'Pay-wise, you were earning a good salary four years ago. James obviously valued you highly.' He hesitated, mentally doubling the amount he'd previously considered and not pausing to think about it—another first— as he made the offer. He watched warm colour stain the high cheekbones, which was reward enough for his magnanimity.

'I— That's— I mean—' Toni pulled herself together. 'That's extremely generous,' she said faintly. Understatement of the year. Was he paying her so much because she'd told him about her debts? Well, she didn't care. She would be able to give her parents board and lodging for herself and the girls and an extra sum for all they would take on now she was working again, and still have a massive amount she could save each month. The debts that had looked to be a millstone round her neck for the next decades would now be able to be dealt with in two or three years if she was frugal. 'Thank you. Thank you so much.'

'Don't thank me too enthusiastically, Toni. I'm a hard taskmaster and you'll earn every penny,' he drawled, only partly tongue in cheek.

She spoke from the heart. 'I don't mind what you ask of me, Mr Landry, and I'll work my socks off. I can promise you that.'

Steel slammed the lid on the reply his suddenly out-of-control libido suggested, keeping his voice bland as he continued, 'The package will include private health insurance for you and immediate family, namely your children in this instance, and a company car will be available when required. You don't have a car of your own, I presume?'

Toni shook her head. It had been tubes and buses lately.

'One last thing. I thought we had progressed to Steel.'

'Oh, yes, of course.' Nervously she ran the tip of her tongue over her lips. 'I'm sorry.'

Steel's eyes followed the motion and again his body reacted in the age-old way. Cursing himself for the ridiculousness of the situation he found himself in, he said quietly, 'I'd like you to take the plans and anything else you need away with you tonight and familiarise yourself with the project before Monday. My secretary will send you a formal offer and all the relevant paperwork tomorrow.'

Toni nodded as Maggie bustled through from the house with their first course. 'Thank you,' she said again.

'Here we are, then.' Maggie placed a plate in front of her as she said, 'I hope you like asparagus, young lady.'

'Yes, I do, and this looks delicious.' The asparagus and ham parcels were covered in a crispy crumb and suddenly Toni was ravenously hungry. They lived up to expectation when she took her first bite; obviously Maggie was a wonderful cook.

'Do you live to eat or eat to live?' Steel asked after a moment or two, his gaze running over her slender shape.

Toni froze for a moment. Naturally slim, she knew

she was too thin at the moment and her clothes were hanging on her and immediately took the question as a subtle criticism. She'd had to alter the waistband of the skirt she had on that morning, and although her white silk shirt was supposed to be loose it didn't fit her as it had when she'd bought it a year ago. Sleepless nights spent worrying over the last four months had taken their toll. She took a sip of champagne and nerved herself to look into the handsome face. 'I like food so I suppose the former. Yes, definitely the former.'

He grinned. 'Me too.'

The beat of sexual awareness that vibrated through her veins almost caused her to drop the champagne flute. Horrified at herself, she prayed frantically he hadn't noticed. It had been that smile, the way it had mellowed the hard planes and angles of his face and crinkled the silver-blue eyes. But he was her boss, well, practically. And she was in his world now. A world where sophisticated, worldly men and women could share a meal and eat and drink and converse as colleagues and nothing more. Besides which, if she ever got involved with another man in the whole of her life it would be too soon. All she wanted was to bring up the girls the best she could after she cleared the mountain of debts Richard had left. They were her life now and there was no room for anyone else, not that a man like Steel Landry would remotely be interested in a widow with two small children in tow.

The conversation was inconsequential while they ate and she found Steel had a wickedly dry wit, his observations on day-to-day life turning fairly mundane happenings into something hysterically funny. He had it all, she thought as she savoured the marinated chilli and ginger steaks Maggie had brought for the next course. Looks, personality, wealth. Women would throw themselves at him till the day he died; he was that sort of man. How would a girlfriend or wife cope with that? They would have to be very sure of their own worth and of him too, but could you ever be sure of someone like Steel Landry?

Dessert was a frothy chocolate concoction with a raspberry sauce that was tangy and complemented the rich chocolate perfectly, and by the end of the meal Toni was very full and more relaxed. But only up to a point. Steel simply wasn't the sort of man you could relax around—or maybe she should say the sort of man *she* could relax around, she acknowledged silently. He was too…disturbing.

Maggie had gone home once she had brought out the dessert and coffee, and now Toni said, 'Maggie's a wonderful cook. Has she worked for you long?'

He nodded. 'A good few years. She comes in most afternoons and prepares an evening meal unless I'm going out, and sees to the apartment and laundry and so on. Her husband died shortly before she came to work for me and left her fairly well off, but she likes to keep busy. She looks after one of her grandchildren every morning so the hours here suit her.'

Toni thought back to the motherly way Maggie had with her. 'She likes to feel needed.'

The observation seemed to surprise him. 'Needed?' He considered this for a moment. 'Yes, I suppose you're right, I hadn't looked at it like that. She was very happily married, by all accounts, so I suppose it must have been hard when her husband died, especially as it was a long illness and she nursed him herself. She's a good person.'

And devoted to Steel, by the way she'd fussed round

him. Which had to mean he wasn't quite the hard, remote, slightly sardonic mogul he presented to the world?

Or maybe it didn't. She didn't know, Toni thought confusedly, what Steel was, and she didn't need to. She was an employee, that was all. She finished the last of her coffee, feeling acutely awkward as she said, 'That was a lovely meal and all the nicer for being so unexpected. Thank you.'

'My pleasure.' The firm, sensual mouth suddenly quirked with amusement as he added, 'See the lengths I've gone to to make you relax?'

She giggled, she couldn't help it, the first real natural response she'd made all evening, then felt acutely embarrassed as the silver eyes narrowed on her mouth.

'That's better,' he murmured, 'but don't tense up on me again. Let's go and sort out those plans and the other bits and pieces before I call a taxi.'

'Oh, you needn't do that,' she said quickly. 'I came by underground and—'

'And you're going home with me in a taxi.'

With him? This was getting worse. 'I've got my ticket—'

'I'm going to call the hospital for an update and then a cab, OK? I have never yet left any young woman I was responsible for to make her own way home, and I don't intend to start with you, Toni.'

She stared at him. 'You're not responsible for me.'

'You came here early this evening because I asked you to and you stayed for a meal for the same reason. It is now—' he consulted his watch '—getting on for eleven, and soon all the gremlins and goblins come out to play. Indulge me.'

He was light-hearted, casual, but she couldn't rise to the humour. 'Really, there's no need.'

'Yes, there is.' The silver eyes fixed her determinedly.

Oh, for goodness' sake! 'Thank you,' she said. Not.

'I'd drive myself but I've had a drink,' he added, rising to his feet as though the matter was settled. 'Now come along.'

Toni stood up. She felt she couldn't do anything else but she found she really didn't want to ride home with him in a taxi. They'd shared a meal, admittedly, but on opposite sides of the table. A taxi was altogether more...She baulked at the word *intimate* and substituted *cosy*.

Fifteen minutes later she was sitting in a cab on her way home to Finsbury clutching her portfolio to her chest. Steel was sprawled beside her taking a good two-thirds of the seat, his long legs stretched in front of him and his whole persona one of lazy relaxation as he went over a few key points of the project.

Toni tried to concentrate, she really did, but she was acutely aware of a hard male thigh against hers, the five-o'clock stubble on his chin, which accentuated his brand of aggressive masculinity tenfold, and, not least, the *bigness* of him. The hard muscled shoulders were broad in keeping with his height, but it was more the overall virility of the man that was so disturbing. And attractive. And definitely scary.

Oh, she didn't doubt those worldly, sophisticated women a man like Steel would date would be able to handle his fascination just fine. But she was neither worldly nor sophisticated, she admitted feverishly, wishing the journey would end. Before Richard she had never slept with a man before. Lots of her boyfriends had tried to go all the way, of course, but that wasn't how she had been brought up. She hadn't minded kissing and petting, she was as red-blooded as the next woman, but she'd always known she would need to be in love before she committed herself body, soul and spirit. It was just the way she was made and that was that. She'd done apologising for the fact long before Richard had come across the horizon. It hadn't taken her long to understand that the male sex worked on quite another agenda, however. Most of them didn't need to do more than like a woman before they indulged in anything and everything, no holds barred. And some of them simply refused to compute the word *no.*

But Richard had been understanding and prepared to wait. He'd assured her that one-night stands and casual sex weren't on his agenda either, and he had charmed her down the aisle before she had recognised he was essentially a terribly weak and flawed individual. But even then, when her love had turned to lukewarm affection and she had realised she was always going to have to be the strong one in the relationship, the one who carried the family and made all the important decisions, she still hadn't known about his addiction. He had been cunning enough to keep that dark side of his life from her completely, so maybe he had been stronger than she'd thought?

To her acute discomfort she came out of the maelstrom of memories to find Steel was watching her with eyes like polished, razor-sharp crystal. 'I'm sorry?' Too late she realised he was waiting for an answer to a question she hadn't heard. Wonderful. Just the way to show a new boss you were on the ball.

'It doesn't matter.' He brushed away whatever he'd said with an inclination of his head, but his gaze didn't leave her face as he continued, 'What were you thinking about just now?'

She had only known him a matter of hours but she already knew prevarication wasn't an option. Deciding a half-truth would carry the weight she needed, she said quietly, 'I was thinking how someone's life can be turned around in an hour or two. When I came to see you tonight the future looked like an uphill struggle I might never get control of, but now, now I feel I've been given my life back. Richard left us in a terrible mess and it was hard to come to terms with the fact I'd never really known him in spite of being married for four years. But that is the past and I have to look to the future for me and the girls. I can do that now.'

He was still watching her closely but his tone was light when he said, 'What would you have done if I hadn't offered you the job?'

She shrugged. 'Picked myself up and carried on.'

'The English bulldog we-will-not-be-beaten spirit?'

It was faintly mocking and, as had happened more than once that evening, he'd caught her on the raw. 'No,' she answered steadily, 'just the spirit of a mother who is determined to make a good life for her children, that's all. Whatever it takes.'

'A mother.' His eyes ran over her for a second, and although she had her coat on she felt her breasts tingle as though he had reached out and touched her. 'I find it difficult to see you as a mother. Not that I doubt you're a very good one,' he added hastily, 'but you look so young and—' his tone changed, becoming self-derisive '—untouched.'

'Looks are deceptive.' His brief inspection had left her feeling panicky and afraid of something she couldn't put a name to. And it was because of this she felt compelled to add, 'I am totally a mother; Amelia and Daisy are the only people who really matter to me and that's the way it's going to be from now on. We don't need anyone else.'

'I'm sure your parents would be gratified to hear that,' he murmured drily, one dark eyebrow quirking.

'I didn't mean them. I meant...'

'I think I know what you meant,' he put in soothingly as her voice dwindled away. 'You intend to devote yourself to your children and your work. Is that right?'

She nodded. She felt he was laughing at her but the handsome, hard face was giving nothing away.

'You don't think life might be a little...dull after a while?'

The last four years were suddenly stark and sharp on the screen of her mind. The grind, the agonising, the turmoil of making an unworkable marriage work for the sake of the twins. She had gritted her teeth and fulfilled her wifely duties in bed and out of it, but all the time she'd known she was living a lie. Richard had worked impossibly long hours and when he'd arrived home he'd been difficult and sometimes downright hostile, not wanting anything to do with Amelia and Daisy. Of course she knew now that was mostly due to the gambling. The long hours at 'work', the family occasions he'd missed and times he'd let her down when they'd had guests to dinner and he hadn't come home; all the time he'd been feeding his addiction. She had told herself he was putting in the hours for them, her and the children, and stomached it all, tolerating his moods and rages. What a fool she had been. What a gullible, blind fool. But never again. Never, ever again.

Looking straight into the silver-blue eyes, she said, 'I

don't mind dull at all, as it happens, as long as Amelia and Daisy are happy and healthy.'

They had just drawn up outside her parents' terrace, and even in the dark it was clear how small and narrow the houses were. Toni felt a fleeting stab of embarrassment when she remembered the sumptuous penthouse and then she told herself not to be such a snob. It didn't matter what Steel thought and her parents' home was perfect for a retired elderly couple. It was just unfortunate it had been forced to stretch to include herself and the girls too.

'Thank you, Mr—Steel,' she corrected quickly when one dark eyebrow rose. 'I'll see you Monday morning and I'll have some ideas and prices sketched out by then.'

He moved to open the door and stepped out of the cab, holding out his hand to help her descend into the street. He didn't let go of her fingers once she was standing in front of him, shaking her hand as he said, 'Goodnight, Toni. I'm sure you're going to be an asset to the business. Welcome on board.'

'Thank you,' she said again. His flesh was firm and warm and he seemed to tower over her, his gaze all-encompassing. She suddenly realised with a little shock of awareness that she was frightened of him. She didn't want this job, wonderful as it was. Not if it meant working closely with Steel Landry. But she couldn't refuse such an opportunity either. She didn't need to be told it was the chance of a lifetime, a one-off opening into a world where the sky was the limit. And he had been kind, she told herself in the next moment. And a perfect gentleman. She was just being silly.

'Goodnight,' he said again. 'Sleep well.'

Too late she realised she'd been standing gazing at

him like a rabbit frozen in front of a car's headlights, and he had let go of her hand, obviously expecting her to walk away. Blushing furiously, she managed a somewhat strangled, 'Goodnight,' and made her escape, fumbling in her bag for her key as she walked across the pavement and mounted the two steps to the door and then almost dropping the key in her haste.

As the door opened she heard the taxi door slam, but when she turned around it hadn't moved away. She raised a self-conscious hand and then shut the door, leaning against it as she listened to the cab drive off. Her heart was thudding like a drum and she had a feeling she could only describe as panic. She held a hand to her chest, shutting her eyes.

It was a minute or two before her breathing steadied and she straightened. The house was quiet; clearly her parents had retired for the night and just left the hall and landing lights on. She walked through to the small kitchen and dining room at the back of the house, dumping her portfolio and the plans and other bits and pieces on the table before opening the French doors that led into her parents' tiny square of garden. This had originally been a backyard with an outside lavatory when the Victorian terrace was first constructed; now most of the householders had done the same as her parents and converted the space into a paved patio surrounded by potted plants and leafy ferns where they could enjoy a meal alfresco.

Toni sat down on one of the pretty wrought-iron chairs, resting her elbows on the table as she massaged tense muscles at the back of her neck. The tiny space trapped any warmth in the air during the day, making it very pleasant come nightfall, and the heady perfume from the white lilies and clematis and little geraniums with brown and green striped flowers that smelled of cloves and limes from dusk till dawn gradually relaxed her senses. She shut her eyes, lifting her face up to the black night sky in which a million stars twinkled.

Why had Steel Landry affected her so badly? It wasn't like her to be so skittish or given to fancies; she was normally down-to-earth and logical. When she thought about it her circumstances had changed dramatically in the last few hours; she ought to be down on her bended knees thanking God for him, not quibbling about whether to take the job or not. Thanks to him, in a year or two she could envisage affording a proper family home for the girls, somewhere like this little house where the three of them could be happy. A mortgage on a little terrace with a small outside place for the girls to play wouldn't be beyond her and would be far better than a bedsit or flat for the twins. Paying for after-school care until she was home; continuing the girls' ballet lessons, which they'd adored and had to give up after Richard's death; holidays—suddenly they were all on the agenda again.

Toni hugged herself, a dart of joy causing her to smile. It was all going to be all right, she could get her life on an even keel again and once she'd dealt with the debts she'd feel in control once more. And she'd been ridiculous about Steel. It was just that she'd never met a self-made multimillionaire before, never felt such power and charisma radiating from a mere human being. That was all it was.

She nodded to herself. Poor man, when all he'd done was help her; thank goodness he hadn't been able to read her thoughts.

The 'poor man' was at that moment sitting in the back of the cab having—what was for Steel—the very unusual experience of feeling regret. His mouth set in a grim line, he scowled at the passing scene outside the window as he told himself he'd been crazy to employ Toni George. The smartest thing he could have done was to conduct the interview quickly, let her down gently and show her the door. That way he wouldn't have had to see her again. The last thing, the very last thing he needed was to be lusting after a woman who worked for him; a woman in the throes of coping with the aftermath of what had clearly been an unhappy marriage and who had two small children.

He forced himself to lean back in the seat, unlocking tense muscles one by one. Dammit, she might be beautiful and intelligent and gutsy, but so were thousands of other women out there. He should know—he'd had his fair share of female companions in his time. So what— here the muscles he'd relaxed tightened again—made Toni George different from the rest? Because different she was. In fact he didn't think he'd ever felt such instant desire for a woman before. When he'd seen her standing there silhouetted against the window with the sunshine picking out deep highlights in the dark brown of her hair, his body had felt the impact right down to his toes.

He stared out of the window again but without taking anything in. Business was business. He could have employed any one of a number of interior designers, so what the hell was he doing taking her on when he knew it was going to be a problem for him?

No, no, it wasn't. He wouldn't let it be. He was thirty-eight years old, for crying out loud, not some teenager in the throes of blind passion who let what was between his legs rule his mind.

Not sure whether he was angrier with her for invading

his smoothly controlled world or with himself for the way he'd handled things, he continued to brood as the taxi sped its way through the London streets.

On entering the apartment he went straight into his bedroom and, after stripping off, had a long, cool shower in the en-suite bathroom. It helped. Wrapping a towel round his wet thighs, he padded through to the immaculate kitchen and fixed himself a strong coffee. He had a briefcase of work he'd brought home and he didn't want to go to sleep; Jeff had promised to ring him if there was any change in Annie's condition and he was too on edge to go to bed. Purely with concern for Annie, he added, as though someone had challenged otherwise. Anyway, he only needed three or four hours' sleep a night. He'd always been that way.

With the single-mindedness that his business rivals termed ruthlessness, Steel put all thoughts of Toni George out of his mind and, after pulling on his bathrobe, opened the briefcase. Life—his life—was all about autonomy. Anything or anyone that threatened that hard-won and most precious commodity wasn't to be tolerated.

End of story.

# CHAPTER FOUR

'WELL, HOW DO YOU think Mummy looks?' Toni twirled round for the twins' inspection. 'Neat and efficient?'

'What's *'ficient*?' Daisy asked worriedly.

'Someone who can do things well.'

Amelia's big brown eyes had made a thorough examination of her mother's tailored grey suit and crisp white blouse, and now she nodded along with her sister. 'You look very 'ficient,' she declared positively.

'An' pretty,' put in Daisy. 'Very, *very* pretty.'

'Thank you, my honeybees.' Toni carefully knelt down and the twins hugged her, nearly dislodging the tight chignon at the nape of her neck, which had taken her ages to secure. Her thick hair didn't take kindly to being confined. 'Now Grandma is going to take you to nursery today as it's Mummy's first morning at her new job, but tomorrow and most other days I can take you. OK?'

They nodded again, their brown curls bobbing. Although identical at birth there were definite dissimilarities occurring the older the twins became. Amelia was taller than her sister and altogether more robust-looking, and Daisy's brown hair was becoming a shade or two lighter than her sister's. Facially, though, they were still peas in a pod.

Toni stood up, loving them so much her heart ached and hating to leave them, although the twins seemed unconcerned. They had been going to nursery for the last few months to prepare them for big school in September after their fourth birthday at the end of July, and both girls had settled in well. One good thing that had come out of their father's lack of interest in them was that his passing had affected them less than it would have done if he'd been a hands-on type, Toni reflected, not for the first time. Indeed, they had barely mentioned him in the last month or two, but then perhaps that wasn't so surprising. Sometimes a whole week had passed with Richard leaving the flat before the girls were awake and returning home when they were asleep. He had admitted once, when the girls were still babies, that he didn't like children much, and when she had got upset had promised her that of course that didn't mean his own and he would take more interest in the twins when they were out of the baby stage. But he hadn't. Just the opposite, in fact.

'You look very smart, dear.' Vivienne bustled into the sitting room, her voice brisk and uplifting. She knew how her daughter was feeling. 'And you shouldn't have put away the bed. I can do that when you're gone.'

'It's no trouble.' Toni liked to restore the sitting room to order before her parents rose in the morning; the twins' toys and books and other paraphernalia inevitably seemed to end up all over the house, although she told the girls to keep their things in their bedroom. The least she could do was to remove all evidence of the lodger in the front room! Leaning forward, she kissed her mother's lined cheek, saying softly, 'Thanks for being you, Mum. I don't know what I'd have done without you and Dad in the last months.'

'Go on with you.' Vivienne never did like being thanked, but her voice was tender. Only she knew just how much her daughter had suffered before and after her son-in-law's death, and what a change it had wrought in the trusting, confident young woman Toni had been before Richard had come along. It was awful that her son-in-law's life had been cut short like that, but—and she'd never admit it to a living soul—she had felt an element of relief when she'd heard the news, and that was before they'd found out about his gambling. He would have been a millstone round her daughter's neck all her life, Vivienne thought as she watched Toni say goodbye to the girls, because Toni would never have left him. Till death do us part was just that in her daughter's book.

'Wish me luck, Mum.'

Vivienne smiled at her daughter before giving her a hug. 'You don't need luck. Just be yourself and that will be enough. James said you were the best interior designer he'd ever had working for him, and this Landry fellow was obviously impressed else he'd never have given you the job.'

Toni repeated her mother's words like a mantra all the way to Steel's offices north of Edmonton. She'd received a letter and various correspondence including a contract of employment from Steel's secretary the week before, so once in the impressive reception she gave her name and was directed to the lift, where she travelled to the top floor and knocked on the door marked 'Joy Maclean, Secretary to Steel Landry'.

There was no answer, and when she tentatively opened the door and looked inside the office was empty. Steel's secretary clearly hadn't arrived yet.

She knew she was early. Toni glanced at her watch. It was only eight-twenty but she'd wanted to arrive before the rush. She didn't admit to herself here that the 'rush' translated into her formidable employer.

The secretary's office was large and comfortable, even luxurious, the far wall mostly glass, which gave a panoramic view over greater London, and Toni was wondering whether to venture in and sit and wait when a deep smoky voice some way down the thickly carpeted corridor almost made her jump out of her skin.

'Good morning, Toni.' Steel had opened what was obviously the outer door to his office and was leaning nonchalantly against it, hands thrust in the pockets of his perfectly creased trousers. He was wearing a deep blue shirt and his tie was hanging loose, his shirtsleeves rolled up to expose tanned, muscled forearms. He looked sensational, even better than she remembered. No man should have so much; it wasn't fair.

Somehow she managed a smile although her facial muscles felt as stiff as a board. 'Good morning.'

'Joy's rarely here before nine; I keep her working late most evenings so she arrives when she arrives,' he said lazily.

Flexible working hours, of course. She was dry-mouthed and rooted to the spot and desperately tried to pull herself together. *Say something intelligent,* she told herself. *Speak.*

'Come and have a coffee.' He moved back into his office without waiting for a reply, leaving her with no choice but to walk down the corridor.

Steel's office was massive. A giant desk was positioned so the light from the huge windows streamed over his shoulder, and there were a couple of easy sofas and chairs grouped round an enormous coffee table close to a unit holding a coffee maker, a water filter and what looked like a small fridge. A biscuit tin holding a vast selection of biscuits had its lid off, and he took one as he poured her a coffee.

'Breakfast,' he said wryly, indicating the tin. 'There was a panic over the weekend and I've been here since five o'clock. Joy's bringing some bacon butties with her when she comes in.'

'Five o'clock?' She'd have had to be up with the larks to get here before him then.

He smiled, handing her a cup of coffee. 'Help yourself to milk and sugar, or there's cream in the fridge if you prefer,' he said, before adding, 'Five's OK. I often get here around six anyway. I don't sleep much.'

Superman. Only to be expected really. Why would Steel Landry function like a mere mortal?

He nodded to the plans tucked under her arm. 'Come and sit down and tell me how you've got on,' he said, taking the plans and spreading them out on the coffee table before sitting down on one of the sofas.

Toni looked down on the dark head for a moment. His hair was severely slicked back but a wayward tuft was defying the austere style and attempting to fall forward into a quiff. She felt a trickle of something hot surge through her veins and hastily sat down, so hastily she spilt a few drops of coffee onto the plans. Horrified, she blurted, 'Oh, I'm sorry,' reaching into her handbag and dabbing the drops with a tissue, which only spread the stain further.

'Hey, don't worry.' His hand on her wrist was cool and although the contact only lasted a second she felt the impact for moments afterwards. 'Leave it, it's nothing. I have several other sets anyway. Now, show me what you've done.'

Hot and flustered, she began to speak, wondering what he must be thinking, but after a minute or two she became absorbed in her ideas, enthusiasm steadying her voice. Oblivious to his gaze moving to her animated face now and again, she outlined the different themes to the properties, her manner eager and natural. 'So, what do you think?' she said at last, raising her head and looking straight at him.

What he thought was that he'd like to feel the soft curves of her delectable lips beneath his and free her hair from that bun thing so he could run his fingers through it, Steel told himself ruefully. Hell, he wanted this woman more than he'd wanted anyone for a long, long time.

To give himself a breathing space he stood up and walked over to the coffee machine. 'Another cup?' he asked her, turning slightly. 'I'm afraid I drink this stuff like water.'

'No, I'm fine.'

He poured himself a black coffee and drank it straight down, scalding hot as it was, before saying, 'I'm impressed. You've captured the vision of making each apartment different without any one lording it over another. Important with my clientele—they can be touchy about their status,' he added drily. 'The use of beautiful textiles, bold patterns and the vibrant gemstone-inspired colours will go some way to offset the somewhat utilitarian façade of the building, which cannot be changed to any great degree, but remember in winter the apartments will need to feel cosy with fires and the warmth of wooden floors, and in summer we need to get light flooding in where possible. I presume you have a source for the modern art and some of those more unusual materials and fabrics?'

Toni nodded. 'Several. When I worked for James we had a client who wanted his hotel designed with a modern take on ancient Rajasthani architecture and interior design. It was a fascinating project. He even incorporated a lotus-patterned swimming pool and a bar with a stargazing deck.'

'Our clients will have to make do with their bathrooms and wet room, but I like your idea of iridescent glass mosaic tiles. OK, full steam ahead, Toni.' He saw her cheeks flush pink with pleasure and as she gathered up the plans and drawings he caught a discreet glimpse of creamy cleavage and his body hardened instantly. 'I'll take you to the site later today so you can get a feel for the place, but for now let me show you where you'll be working. For the time being you'll be sharing Joy's office. I trust that's acceptable?'

It was a rhetorical question but Toni answered it anyway, her breathless, 'Of course,' lost as he opened the interconnecting door through to his secretary's office and stood aside for her to precede him. She saw a large desk and chair, a filing cabinet and various items of drawing equipment had been arranged in one half of the room, but even so there was plenty of space. She hoped Joy didn't mind her imposing, though.

Steel glanced at his watch. 'Joy should be here shortly so settle yourself in and she'll tell you what's what.'

'Thank you.'

He leaned against the door, his expression slightly quizzical. 'Don't look so scared,' he said softly. 'I don't know what you've heard about me but I can assure you it's bound to have been grossly exaggerated. I rarely bite.'

Toni reacted immediately, straightening and giving him a cool smile. 'I'm merely a little nervous, as everyone is on the first morning at a new job, and in my case it's been a while since I've had to earn a crust.'

Her tone had his eyes narrowing slightly but he made no comment, merely nodding slowly before shutting the door and leaving her alone.

Toni put her hands to her flushed cheeks. Great start. Offending the boss. She sank down on the comfortable leather chair behind the desk and took stock of her surroundings. This would be a lovely place to work. Her corner of the main office at James's practice had been cramped and on the dark side, as well as noisy. This was altogether different, and she was being paid handsomely to boot. If only Steel were more of an average boss everything in the garden would be coming up smelling of roses. But then, if he were an average kind of guy she wouldn't be sitting in a fabulous office with a terrific project to get her teeth into and with a salary that had caused her mother to sit down suddenly when she'd told her the good news. Steel was larger than life in every respect and she needed to adapt to that and fast. She couldn't keep going to pieces around him or, worse, acting as she had just done when all he'd been trying to do was put her at her ease. If only he weren't so good-looking and aggressively masculine and *big*, she thought despairingly.

And the sexiest man on the planet, another part of her mind added relentlessly, with that certain something that made it impossible to be in his company without wondering what it would be like to be made love to by a man like him.

There, it was out at last—the thought she'd been fighting against admitting since she'd first set eyes on him. And he had been right a minute ago. He *did* scare her. She didn't want to feel attracted to another man for the rest of her life, or certainly a long, long time, and, although she knew there wasn't the remotest chance of anything happening between Steel and herself, it still terrified her she could feel this way.

But this was her problem, not Steel's. She simply couldn't go on being so awkward and jumpy in his presence. To him she was just another employee and she would die, on the spot, if he guessed how she felt. And the irony was that if the impossible happened and he made a move on her she would run a mile. Steel was the last man in the world she'd ever get involved with. Her life was Amelia and Daisy now, and she would never allow a man into their precious threesome. She owed her daughters that at least. They had their grandfather as a stable male influence when one was needed and that was perfect; she could rely on her father not to let the twins down. Anyone else was suspect.

The door opening cut into her thoughts and a tall, slim blonde woman smiled at her, saying, 'You must be Toni? Hi, I'm Joy, Steel's secretary. Nice to meet you.'

The rest of the morning flew by. Joy spent some time showing her where everything was and introducing her around. The top floor of the building housed Steel and Joy's offices, Steel's private bathroom, a large conference room and another cloakroom. The floor below was used by Steel's legal people and the accounts department, and the ground floor consisted of Reception and the team who controlled the outside contractors Steel used for various projects, along with various other employees Toni lost track of. It was a much larger organisation than she had expected but everyone seemed friendly and cheerful.

The two women lunched together in a small bistro-type café a stone's throw from the office, and it was here that Joy filled her in on some facts about their illustrious boss.

'Don't be fooled by the old adage that men can only think of one thing at once, at least not where Steel's concerned,' Joy said, once they'd ordered their soup and rolls. 'He can think of several things at once and he expects everyone else to keep up with him. He's a workaholic but he plays hard too, although he never, *ever* gets seriously involved with a woman. Love 'em and leave 'em, that's Steel's style.'

'The original bachelor?' Toni put in drily.

'And how.' Joy nodded. 'Work is his motivating force; women have to fall into line and accept an affair with him is only semi-permanent and strictly sexual. They queue up for the privilege,' she added wryly. 'And I'm not joking.'

Toni hadn't thought she was.

'He adores his sister though.' Joy spent a few moments explaining how Steel had brought Annie up, finishing with, 'You know she was in danger of losing her baby recently?'

'Uh-huh. How are things?'

'OK. Annie's confined to bed from here on.'

They talked some more and Toni found herself wishing Joy weren't leaving at the end of the summer. She felt the two of them could have become good friends. Joy had already started advertising for her replacement; Steel wanted his new secretary in place long before Joy left so when the time came everything ran as smoothly as he expected.

'Patience is not one of Steel's virtues,' Joy had murmured earlier that morning, eyebrows raised meaningfully, and Toni had nodded that she understood. It wasn't exactly reassuring on her first day when she felt she knew nothing about anything.

Steel had gone out to lunch with a business colleague

and the two women were deep in their respective work when he returned. The interconnecting door opened and he put his head round long enough to say, 'Five minutes and we're leaving for the new site, Toni. Bring the plans and anything else you need.'

She must have looked somewhat alarmed because when the door shut again, Joy said, a touch of laughter in her voice, 'His bark is worse than his bite. He's quite human really.'

Toni smiled weakly and began to collect her things together. She was ready and waiting when Steel buzzed Joy to say he was leaving, and as she joined him in the outside corridor and they walked towards the lift he reached out and took the plans and other data from her, tucking them under his arm. 'Settled in?' he asked briefly, his voice deep and slightly husky in the quiet surroundings as the lift doors glided silently open.

Toni's stomach muscles tightened. Once in the carpeted mirrored box he seemed very close, even though there were a good few inches between them. 'Yes, thank you. Joy's been very kind. She's shown me around and introduced me to everyone.'

'She's a damn good secretary. I'll be sorry to lose her.'

Toni nodded to this, even as she thought, *Joy has worked for you for years. Won't you be sorry to lose* her, *as a person, and not just a secretarial machine?* And then she answered herself immediately. Of course he wouldn't. The smooth running of his precious office was all that mattered; the man was barely human. Perhaps he was really a futuristic robot, a creature from a sci-fi film with the appearance of a flesh and blood man? It would fit in with Joy's warning that he was capable of carrying out a complex series of thoughts and actions simultaneously.

As they exited the lift and walked towards the huge glass doors that led into the street, Toni felt she knew what it was like to be in the presence of royalty. Everyone seemed to stop what they were doing and smile and murmur a 'Good afternoon, sir,' as they passed, and the burly security man in the foyer practically saluted.

'Philip has brought your car round, Mr Landry. He said you didn't want him to chaffeur you this afternoon? I hope that's right?' he added, jumping forward to open the outer doors.

Steel nodded. 'Quite right, Bill. How's the wife? Over that last hospital spell, I hope?'

'She's doing all right, Mr Landry, and still going on about the holiday you sent us on. That week in the sun did her the world of good. Set her up, it did.'

'Good. Glad to hear it.'

They exited the building into the street. A smart young man was standing by a black Aston Martin parked at the kerb, which had the passenger door open. As they walked towards the car Steel murmured, 'Bill's wife's fighting a particularly nasty form of cancer and it's been touch and go a few times. He worships the ground she walks on and they've never had kids, so it's just the two of them. It's hit him hard.'

Toni didn't have a chance to reply before they reached the car. The young man helped her into the leather-clad interior while Steel walked round the gleaming bonnet to the driver's side.

It was just as well she had a few moments to collect herself; his kindness to the security man had thrown her completely. She wouldn't have put Steel Landry down as a philanthropist in any way, shape or form. First mistake, then, and probably not her last.

The man was an enigma, she told herself crossly. He wouldn't stay in the box she'd parcelled him up in in her mind. Which was unsettling. And then she was even more unsettled when he slid into the low sleek car, so close the faint, delicious smell of him swamped her senses. He reached round and threw the plans and other documents into the back seat, his shoulder brushing hers and causing a chain reaction right down to her toes.

'OK?' He gave her a brief smile, clearly not requiring an answer before he started the car and pulled out almost immediately into the London traffic.

She wouldn't have said OK, no, Toni thought wryly. Taking a deep breath, she composed herself and tried to concentrate on anything rather than the hard male body at the side of her. It wasn't easy. In fact it was impossible and as closing her eyes wasn't an option she did the next best thing and stared determinedly out of the side window until she had control of her breathing.

They had only travelled a couple of miles when the car's Bluetooth phone system cut into the tense—at least Toni felt it was tense—silence. It was a business call, and Steel had barely finished speaking before the phone rang again. It set the tone for the journey.

Did he ever stop working? Toni asked herself as Steel manoeuvred the powerful car in and out of the heavy London traffic while discussing facts and figures as decisively as though he were sitting at his desk with the relevant papers in front of him. But then she knew the answer to that; Joy had told her he played as hard as he worked.

She closed her mind to that particular avenue of thought before it took hold. Over the last few nights she'd had one or two particularly erotic dreams, which had been embarrassing to recall in the light of day. And they'd all featured Steel. Thank goodness he'd never know. A little frisson of horror at the notion he might suspect she'd fantasised about him—albeit subconsciously, which was hardly her fault—slivered down her spine. This was so unlike her, it really was.

A good few miles—and a good few phone calls—later, Steel pulled into a parking space in front of a huge, somewhat grim-looking factory building, which still had 'E. C. Maine & Son, Quality Furnishings' over the massive arched front doors. 'I think the most you can say about the exterior is that it looks solid,' Steel murmured wryly. 'I doubt we can do much there.'

'Oh, I don't know...' Toni gazed up at the seemingly hundreds of small windows. 'We've already got permission to join some of the windows together to make large, more attractive ones and they'd look great with outside shutters to break up the brickwork. And look at the detail above the windows; the Victorians did that sort of thing so well. If we follow that through with the alterations and pick out some of the brick patterns with gold and black paint, just above the windows and nowhere else, I think it might look quite charming.'

Steel nodded. 'I see what you mean.'

'And the yard at the back which is going to become the communal garden could be enclosed with ornamental iron railings augmented with the same design to tie in with the building.'

'I like that.' He smiled. 'I like that very much. Do it.'

His approval brought pink into her cheeks but Steel was already striding up to the main doors. By the time he had unlocked them and stood aside for Toni to precede him into the old fusty factory she had gained control.

Seeing the building in its raw state made the project come alive. Carried along on a wave of enthusiasm, Toni found it easier to concentrate on the job in hand and ignore the attraction of the tall dark man prowling about at her side. She was full of ideas, some practical and some not so practical, but by the time they left she knew she could make each apartment spectacular. Initially the vast basement had been designed as a caretaker's flat, but on seeing it Toni had suggested a much smaller, more compact one-bedroomed dwelling with the remaining space kitted out as a gym with sauna and steam rooms for the occupants of the apartments. 'And a jacuzzi,' she'd added, after Steel had approved the idea. 'For the ladies.'

One dark eyebrow quirked. Steel turned from locking the front doors, a lazy smile twisting the stern mouth. 'That's a little sexist,' he protested mildly. 'Males like jacuzzis too.'

'Not as much as women do.'

Steel shrugged, his silver-blue eyes watching the way the evening sunshine brought out the red in her dark brown hair. It was natural, he'd swear to it, he thought inconsequentially. When had he last seen a beautiful woman with hair that owed nothing to a bottle for its rich colour? 'Don't the pins and what have you in that thing make your head ache?' he said suddenly, nodding at her tightly secured coil of hair.

She stared at him as if he'd gone mad—and perhaps he had, Steel thought ruefully. Personal remarks to employees weren't his style.

'A little, perhaps,' she said slowly after a moment or two. 'But it's neat and out of the way for work.'

Steel glanced at his watch. 'It's nearly half-past five. You're officially in your own time.' He could hear himself speaking but didn't seem able to stop himself.

If she understood she didn't give any sign of it. 'I can sketch out some of our new ideas and have them ready for you in the morning.' Her voice was cool, business-like. 'Of course the cost will be pretty general at this stage.'

Damn the ideas. His body had been throbbing with sexual frustration all afternoon and now he gritted his teeth as he walked to the Aston Martin and opened the passenger door, helping her into the car. 'There's no rush.' He leant one arm on the roof of the car and smiled at her. 'Leave them till tomorrow. Fancy a drink now the working day is done?'

What are you *doing*? another part of his brain ground out. You're breaking every rule in the book.

Ah, but they were *his* rules. He was the boss. He could break them if he chose to do so. Anyway, what was the matter in two working colleagues enjoying an end-of-day drink?

She seemed a little flustered but her voice was firm when she said, 'Thank you, but no, I ought to get home. The girls will be having their bath soon and I like to be there when I can.'

Steel blinked, disconcerted to find he'd forgotten her children existed in the last few minutes. 'No problem.' He shut her door, mentally kicking himself as he walked round the bonnet.

When he slid into the car he saw she was sitting very straight and still. He cursed silently. During the afternoon she had relaxed with him and now they were back to square one. 'How about I take you straight home

now, unless you need to call in the office for anything?'
he suggested quietly. 'That way you shouldn't miss time
with your children.'

She glanced at him and he saw her eyes were wary.
'Thank you,' she said after a moment or two. He got the
feeling she would have liked to refuse the offer and wondered why. Was she bothered about what the neighbours
would think when she was brought home in a nice car
by a strange man, or didn't she want to run the risk he
might meet her family? Neither reason sat well and he
felt an edge of anger to his curiosity about what made
this dark-eyed, honey-skinned woman tick.

Toni sat hugging the folder of plans and her notes to
her chest during the journey as though she needed their
protection. Steel wondered what she'd do if he suddenly
pulled into a quiet side road and cut the engine, and
toyed with doing just that to see her reaction for a second
before he had the grace to feel ashamed of himself. But
she made him want to do something outrageous, he told
himself in justification for his crassness. She was so in
command of herself, so restrained. She made him feel
like one of the lecherous villains from the old silent
movies. He could understand why her opinion of the
male sex was at an all-time low, but did she seriously
think he was so boorish as to make a move on her in
his car of all places?

The thought of having her in the back seat, of making
her shake and shiver and moan beneath him as his hands
and mouth explored every inch of her delectable body,
nearly caused him to drive into a large family saloon.
After this Steel gave all his attention to the rush-hour
traffic and let his self-induced arousal subside.

When he drew up outside the terraced house where

her parents lived Toni opened the door even as he cut the engine. 'Wait, I'll help you,' he offered as she began to scramble out of the car, but by the time he'd walked round to her the inevitable had happened and the plans and papers were all over the pavement.

He bent to help her retrieve them, wincing as their heads collided and then catching her as she stumbled.

'I'm so sorry.' She was scarlet. 'It's your car, it's so low.' And then she blushed still more if that was possible.

He thought it showed remarkable restraint when he didn't point out that if she had waited as he'd suggested there wouldn't have been a problem. He managed a creditable laugh. 'I'll use the four-by-four next time.'

'No, I didn't mean—'

She was still in his arms and every muscle in his body had tightened as evidence of the fact. He looked down at her face, noticing a tiny indentation in her nose—the result of an injury when she was young maybe?—and the way her full lips were slightly apart showing small white teeth. He wondered what she tasted like. Sweet as honey. Without a doubt.

It took more will power than he knew he possessed to resist kissing her, to resist plunging his tongue into the moist, undefended territory of her mouth. He wanted her so badly he was in danger of shaking with the need. The scent of her was warm and inviting, teasing his nostrils, and her hair smelt of summer fruit—peaches, apples perhaps.

He straightened, letting his arms fall to his sides and taking a step away from her before he gave in to the sensual desire turning his blood to liquid fire. She didn't move, staring at him with huge eyes, her body as still as his. How long they would have stood there he didn't know, but when the front door to the house opened and shrill shrieks of 'Mummy!' broke the unnatural silence that had fallen she reacted with a speed that took him by surprise. One moment she was staring at him with great dark eyes, the next she was meeting the two little girls who ran pell-mell towards her with outstretched arms.

Steel found he was transfixed. It was an effort to raise his gaze to the stout, grey-haired woman in the doorway who called, 'I'm sorry, dear, but they've been watching from their bedroom window for you to come home and once they caught sight of you...'

'It's all right, Mum.' Toni disentangled herself, turning to Steel with a strained smile as she said, 'These are my children, Amelia and Daisy.'

He'd been right with his second guess. She hadn't wanted him to meet her children. The knowledge hit at the same time as he acknowledged he was experiencing a feeling of tremendous relief that the twins were tiny copies of their mother, apart from their hair, which was a riot of tight brown curls. He couldn't see any obvious evidence of the man who had sired them.

'Hello, Amelia and Daisy,' he said smilingly. 'Who is who?' He crouched down to make himself less intimidating.

'I'm Amelia. She's Daisy.'

One of the twins was burying her face in her mother's neck but the other little girl surveyed him with the penetrating, steady gaze of a child as she spoke. Steel nodded at the tiny figure. 'My name's Steel Landry, Amelia.'

'Steel?' The minute nose wrinkled. 'That's not a name, that's what things are made out of.'

'It's what I'm made out of,' he counteracted swiftly as Toni murmured an agonised *'Amelia'*.

'Like a robot?' Amelia asked interestedly.

'Sort of.' Steel found himself laughing.

The little girl thought for a moment, then she said, 'There's a boy at nursery, his name's Tyler, and he's always picking on Daisy. If I tell him my mummy's got a friend who's made of steel I bet he won't pick on her again.'

'It's worth a try,' said Steel seriously.

Amelia beamed. 'I'll tell him tomorrow.'

'Hello, Mr Landry.' Toni's mother tottered towards him, holding out her hand. 'It's very nice to meet you. Can I offer you a coffee? My husband's just made a fresh pot.'

Toni was looking at her mother and he could see her rejection of the idea on her face before she had time to hide it. It was the spur he needed to answer, 'That would be most welcome. Thank you. If you're sure it's no trouble.'

*Crazy.* As he followed the women and children into the house Steel knew he was playing with fire. This was a woman with more baggage than royalty travelled with, but it didn't make any difference. It should have; everything in his orderly, controlled life to date was screaming that fact at him. But it didn't. He wanted to see her in her natural habitat and the fascination wouldn't be denied. He might regret it—he very probably would, he acknowledged wryly, but he hadn't got to where he was today without taking chances.

He needed to—he *had to*—peek under the façade Toni presented to the world and see *her*, the real woman. He'd ached with a combination of lust and uncertainty since the first moment he'd laid eyes on her and that just wasn't the way he was made. He was a mature, experienced man, rational and logical, even sagacious. He didn't do reckless and impetuous, he told himself again.

'Are you very old?'

Amelia faced him in the small narrow hall and, somewhat taken aback, Steel murmured, 'Not *very* old, no.'

'My grandad is. He's got white hair. When he came to our sports day last week he couldn't run in the fathers' race and Tyler said he was rubbish.'

Steel found he didn't like this Tyler very much.

'Amelia, that's enough.' Toni's face was burning. 'I want you and Daisy to go up and get ready for your bath and I'll come up in a minute. OK? Go on, scoot.'

Steel found himself practically pushed through a door that led to a compact little kitchen and dining room, then out into a patio area where a tall, slightly stooped man rose to shake his hand. 'I'm Toni's father, Mr Landry. William Otley. Do sit down. I normally have a cup of coffee out of the way here while the twins get ready for bed. I find I'm in great need of the caffeine.' He grinned. 'I'm not as young as I used to be.'

Steel smiled back. 'I can imagine they keep you on your toes.'

'Oh, yes, but I wouldn't miss a minute.' Toni was hovering at their side and now her father turned to her. 'Go and see to the girls, dear. I'll look after Mr Landry.'

Her hesitation was visible. She clearly wanted him anywhere but here, Steel thought grimly.

She gave him a hunted smile, murmuring something about she wouldn't be long, and then reluctantly went back into the house.

Steel smiled faintly to himself. Whether she liked it or not she wasn't indifferent to him as a man; the way she had stilled in his arms had told him that. It was a start.

Yes, another part of his mind answered wryly. But a start to what?

## CHAPTER FIVE

'YOU SHOULDN'T HAVE asked him in for coffee.' Toni fairly hissed the words in her mother's ear as they presided over the girls' undressing. 'You really shouldn't have.'

'Why ever not, dear?' Vivienne said airily.

'He's my boss. It's just not...done.'

'Nonsense.' Vivienne whisked Daisy up into her arms.

Toni gave her mother a helpless glance and then decided not to pursue the conversation, aware of little ears flapping. Determined she was still going to put the girls to bed—Steel had known what she intended when he'd accepted her mother's invitation after all—she sent her mother downstairs and supervised the twins' bath time. Once they were in their pyjamas, looking impossibly angelic with flushed cheeks and tousled curls, Amelia declared she wanted to go downstairs to say goodnight to the steel man. 'I want to see him, Mummy. Just for a minute?'

Toni kept her voice bright and pleasant when she said, 'He's talking to Grandad, honeybee, so maybe another time.'

'Ple-e-e-ase, Mummy? Please.'

Daisy glanced from her twin to her mother and then

added her own plea, tugging on Toni's skirt. 'Me too, Mummy. Me too.'

As they'd been speaking Toni had heard her mother coming upstairs. Vivienne had obviously caught the gist of what they'd been saying as she now put her head round the door, saying, 'I can take them down.'

The twins, sensing an ally in their grandmother, increased their entreaties. '*Please*, Mummy. Just for a little while.'

Toni found she was hanging onto her patience by a thread. She didn't want her children getting to know Steel, or any other man for that matter; her home was a place apart from the world outside its four walls. But that was the rub. This wasn't her home, it was her parents', and her mother had every right to invite whomsoever she liked in for coffee.

Was she being ridiculous and churlish? she asked herself wearily, knowing the answer was in the affirmative. Sighing, she said to the two little faces looking up at her so imploringly, 'Just a quick goodnight, then, I mean it, and then I'll read you a story in bed before you settle down.'

The twins shot off, Vivienne following more slowly with Toni bringing up the rear. When she walked out to the patio it was to see Daisy—shy, timid little Daisy—standing in front of Steel with one small hand resting on his knee as she told him some story or other about what had happened at nursery that day. 'An' Miss Brown told him to come back an' say sorry but he wouldn't, would he, Melia?'

Amelia, who was sitting on her grandfather's knee, shook her damp curls. 'He put his tongue out at Miss Brown,' she volunteered.

'An' that's very naughty, isn't it?' Daisy said indignantly.

Steel nodded seriously. 'Very, I'd say.'

'Tyler?' Toni asked over her daughter's head.

'The very same,' Steel said solemnly.

Daisy looked up at her mother. 'He put a flutterby—'

'A butterfly,' Amelia corrected. 'They're called butterflies.'

'He put a butterfly in the crayon tin an' wouldn't let it out an' tried to kick me when I got the lid off an' it flew away.'

'You did that?' asked Toni, amazed. Daisy was frightened of Tyler; all the children were. 'You got the tin away from him?'

Daisy nodded vigorously. 'It was only a little one an' it was scared. It wanted its mummy.'

Toni touched her child's curls. 'That was a kind thing to do, my sweet, but now this mummy wants both her little girls tucked up in bed, so say goodnight to Grandma and Grandad and Mr Landry. Quickly now.'

Daisy ran to her grandfather and he gave both little girls a kiss and then Vivienne did the same; when they reached Steel they clearly expected him to follow suit and he didn't disappoint them. Toni's heart seemed to stop beating for a moment as he bent forward, tenderly kissing each small forehead as he said, 'Goodnight, Amelia. Goodnight, Daisy. I hope Tyler behaves himself tomorrow.'

'He won't,' said Amelia, turning as Toni led the girls away.

'He never does,' added Daisy, beaming at Steel, who smiled back. 'Miss Brown says he's got ants in his pants.'

The twins were asleep even before Toni finished

reading the story they'd chosen, but she continued to sit for a moment in the quiet room, faint echoes of conversation and laughter from the garden drifting up to her. She felt so het up her nerves were stretched to breaking point and her stomach was in knots, and yet really nothing was wrong. Her mother had invited her boss in for a coffee when he'd been nice enough to drop her home. What was wrong with that?

Nothing and everything. When the boss was Steel Landry.

She'd just stepped onto the small landing when her mother came upstairs. Toni took one look at Vivienne's face and said, 'What? What have you done, Mum?' as her stomach plummeted.

'Now don't be cross, dear, but I've asked Steel if he'd like to stay for a bite to eat,' Vivienne said defensively.

Toni said nothing; she couldn't. Words had failed her.

'It was only polite, after all. He must have been able to smell the beef casserole I've got in the oven and there's plenty. He was only going to go back to an empty apartment, bless him, and a man should come home to a hot meal in the evening.'

*Bless him?* 'He's got a daily who sees to the apartment and his meals, Mum,' Toni hissed through gritted teeth. 'He's not little orphan Annie.'

'Talking of Annie,' Vivienne continued, completely undeterred by her daughter's simmering fury, 'he was telling your father and I about his sister. He thinks the world of her, doesn't he? And he must be worried to death. That man's got a lot on his shoulders, Toni. Offering him a meal after how good he's been to you was the least we could do.'

Toni gave up. She didn't know what had been said downstairs, but for some reason her mother had decided Steel was in need of comfort and sustenance. Anyway, it was too late now. The deed was done. Trying to keep her voice from betraying just how angry with her mother she was, she muttered, 'What did he say when you asked him?' as it dawned on her Steel had been put in a very awkward position. He'd probably only accepted the offer of a cup of coffee to be polite, and now here was her mother pressing him to stay for a meal. Would he think she was in cahoots with her mother, that she was attempting to inveigle her way in with the boss by the back door? Worse, would he suspect she fancied him and had asked her mother to pave the way? Joy had said women fell over themselves to sleep with him. Would he assume she was prepared to assume the role of much more than his interior designer?

'What did he say?' Vivienne wrinkled her brow. 'Something about he wouldn't like to impose, I think, but I told him there was no question of that and we'd love him to stay.'

Toni groaned. 'Mum, he was trying to say no.'

'Nonsense, dear. He was just being polite.'

'You probably totally embarrassed him.'

'Of course I didn't.' Vivienne's tone was sharper; she couldn't see what all the fuss was about. He'd looked so pleased when she'd asked him, poor soul. 'You weren't there, Toni, so don't make assumptions. I'm going down to put a few more new potatoes on to go with the casserole, so if you want to change and come down in a minute, you can open a bottle of wine. All right?' And with that Vivienne sailed off, bristling under her daughter's criticism, her grey curls bobbing with righteous indignation.

Toni shut her eyes for a moment. Somehow she had been manoeuvred into the most ridiculous position; she could strangle her mother. This was so *embarrassing.*

Tiptoeing back into the girls' room, she opened the wardrobe, which held some of her things along with a selection of the girls' clothes. The rest of their clothes were packed in two enormous suitcases under the girls' beds; there simply wasn't room for them anywhere else.

The June evening was warm but, in view of her earlier thoughts, she didn't intend to dress up in one of the floaty summer dresses she had. Steel might already have the wrong idea about her; she wasn't about to confirm she was trying to seduce him. With this in mind she pulled on a pair of casual white linen trousers and a sleeveless tunic in a soft jade colour, brushing out her hair and leaving it loose about her shoulders after she had cleaned her face free of make-up. Part of her was itching to put on some mascara and lip gloss as she surveyed her scrubbed, squeaky-clean image in the bathroom mirror, but she resisted the temptation. She was not going to titivate in the slightest; just the opposite, in fact.

Thrusting her feet into a pair of old flip-flops, she went downstairs, so nervous she had to pause in the hall and unclench her fingers, which were in tight fists at her side.

Her mother had clearly already opened the bottle of wine. When she walked through to the patio Steel and her parents were deep in conversation, a bottle of red on the table and four wine glasses half full. The somnolent air was rich with the scents from the potted plants and herbs that were her father's pride and joy, and as she paused in the doorway the three of them laughed at something that had been said. There was a naturalness to the scene, an easy-going atmosphere that made Toni feel all at odds with the others. They seemed to know each other and yet they'd only just met; it was silly but she felt horribly left out and almost betrayed, as if Steel Landry had intruded into that part of her life she had to keep separate from any outside influences.

Steel looked up and saw her. His hand had been reaching for his wine glass and it paused momentarily, his crystal eyes narrowing. Then his fingers closed round the stem and his voice was smoky when he said, 'Toni, we were wondering where you'd got to. Come and sit down and have a glass of wine.'

His words reinforced the strange feeling but also provided the shot of adrenaline she needed to walk out into the evening air with a polite smile on her face. 'I hear my mother's roped you in for a meal,' she said coolly. 'I hope that won't upset Maggie if she's got one of her wonderful dinners prepared.'

The thick black lashes swept down to hide the expression in his eyes for a moment. 'Maggie's away for a couple of days,' he said smoothly, his gaze encompassing Vivienne and William as he added, 'We all need a break now and again.'

'Absolutely.' Vivienne sent a triumphant glance her daughter's way. 'I'm sure she'd be glad to know you're having a hot meal.'

Her father's look was more of a reproof, stating—as if she didn't know—that she was being uncharacteristically rude to a guest. Feeling as though she were a recalcitrant child who had been put in her place, Toni reached for her glass of wine. In all her wildest dreams she hadn't expected her first day at work to end like this, she thought with a faint touch of hysteria.

They ate at the small patio table, which was disturbingly cosy. Her mother's casserole followed by sherry trifle couldn't compete with Maggie's culinary expertise, but Steel further endeared himself to Vivienne by having second helpings of everything and declaring every mouthful delicious.

Toni struggled to eat anything. If it weren't for the effect he had on her; if the owner of Landry Enterprises had been an elderly, white-haired gentleman or a geek type or even a Flash Harry, she would have handled this situation perfectly well, but Steel...Steel was Steel. Devastatingly attractive and every bit as dangerous; more powerful and sure of himself than anyone she'd met and a man who had a different woman for every day of the week, if half the rumours about him were to be believed. And she believed them, every one of them. Look how he had her mother eating out of his hand; her father too, come to it.

When her mother bustled inside to fix some coffee, refusing Toni's offer of help with a cheery, 'I can manage perfectly well, dear,' a soft twilight was falling, bathing the tiny garden in scented intimate shadows. It was a beautiful evening, the sort of night when lovers would take a long slow walk along country lanes wrapped in each other's arms, Toni thought with a pang of longing, before silently chastising herself for such a notion. Whatever was the matter with her?

But she didn't need to ask. She had never been so aware of another human being in her life as she was of Steel tonight. Every slight movement he'd made, every intonation of his voice had shot along her nerves like liquid fire. The breadth of his shoulders outlined under his shirt—his jacket long since having been discarded—the sculptured bone structure and hard handsome face, and not least the big predatory male body had dried her mouth and caused her heart to palpitate. And over and over had drummed the thought that she had committed herself to working with this man, that he was her *boss*, that she couldn't escape him. And would she want to, even if she could?

'I'm just going to get my pipe and baccy.' Her father ambled to his feet and Toni had to resist the urge to grab hold of him and demand he stay as she watched him enter the house.

'Don't worry, you're not alone with me.' Steel's voice held dark amusement and as her eyes shot to his face he nodded at the high brick wall dividing the gardens. A small robin was perched there surveying them with bright black eyes, head slightly on one side. 'We have a chaperone on hand.'

'Don't be silly, I'm not worried,' she lied quickly. 'I'm just embarrassed my mother wouldn't take no for an answer when she suggested you stay for dinner. She's never worked outside the home, you see. She's got no idea of how things are done in the modern world. She still operates half a century behind the times, I'm afraid.'

'Don't apologise for her, she's great, and for the record I had no intention of saying no when she asked.' He settled back in his chair, his eyes pure mother-of-pearl in the fading light. 'I wanted to stay.'

'Oh.' Taken aback at his frankness, Toni nodded helplessly. 'I see.'

'I doubt it.' There was lingering amusement in the curl of his mouth, but he didn't elaborate, instead continuing, 'Amelia and Daisy are delightful. They're a credit to you.'

'Thank you.' She had stiffened slightly as he spoke.

'Very different personalities; almost like the two halves which make up their mother.'

She was taking a sip of wine, but was surprised into looking at the pearly eyes. She couldn't resist asking, 'What does that mean?'

'One so sure of herself and how she sees the world; a go-getter with boundless enthusiasm and a zest for life. The other more shy and vulnerable, needing to know she's safe and secure, holding on to what she knows because she's afraid of getting hurt.'

Toni stared at him, a hot prickly sensation running up and down her spine as she saw he was perfectly serious. His insight unnerved her totally and to combat the weakness she took refuge in a feigned cynicism, managing a scornful little smile before she said, 'And you saw all that in two little girls in, what—five minutes? I hardly think so.'

'You're telling me I'm wrong?' His voice was mild, reasonable.

'Of course, Amelia and Daisy are much more complex than that.'

'I wasn't talking about the twins.'

Toni took a deep breath. He was her boss and she needed this job, but she was blowed if she was putting up with whatever game he was playing. 'Don't attempt to analyse me when you've hardly spent any time in my company,' she said tightly.

He didn't seem the least offended. In fact he smiled, the hard angles of his face breaking up into attractive curves. 'Fair enough,' he said silkily, 'but I know I'm right. Tonight you look about sixteen, do you know that? And infinitely more lovely than the capable career woman of daylight hours. I thought at first that I was seeing you with the outer shell removed, but that's not true, is it? It's still there, it's just taken a different form.

What would it take for you to relax, really relax in a man's company, Toni?'

She cleared her dry throat. 'I haven't the faintest idea what you're talking about.'

'At work you're a remarkably gifted and enterprising woman, one who isn't afraid to take chances and think outside the box. And such enthusiasm is catching. You've certainly excited me,' he said, deadpan, before adding, 'I can't wait to see the finished apartments in due course.'

She stared at him, flustered and confused. When he'd said she excited him for a moment she'd thought… But he hadn't meant *she* excited him, she told herself in a hot flush of embarrassment at her ridiculous assumption. Merely that her plans for the apartments did. She had to get a hold of herself around this man.

'But then the other side of you is incredibly wary and suspicious,' he went on softly, 'which is perfectly understandable after all that's happened.'

Her chin rose. 'I'm not wary and suspicious. That's nonsense. I admit I'm very aware of being a single mother with two small children depending on me, and I certainly don't intend to be the sort of woman who introduces a succession of "uncles" to them either. That simply won't happen, now or in the future.'

'I'm glad to hear it,' he said solemnly.

Her lips tightened. Was he laughing at her? Anger made her speak before she thought as she bit out, 'And we're better off keeping it to just the three of us. I won't allow them to be let down again. We're perfectly happy just as we are.'

'You love them very much,' he stated quietly. 'Don't you?'

'They are everything to me and I to them. It's always been that way since they were born.'

'And their father? Where did he fit in?'

Not sure if she sensed criticism, she glared at him. 'You needn't feel sorry for Richard. He wanted nothing to do with the girls. I didn't shut him out or anything.'

'I didn't say I felt sorry for him, I asked where he fitted in. That's quite different.'

Yes, it was, and she didn't know why every word he said caught her on the raw. She swallowed hard. 'I'm sorry, I thought...' She looked away but the robin had gone. She really was on her own with him now. Gathering her thoughts, she said flatly, 'Richard was the sort of man who should never have fathered children. He didn't like them. It was as simple as that. He had no time for little ones, none at all.'

'Not even his own?'

If she hadn't been so tense she would have smiled at the incredulity in his voice. 'Not really. We knew each other for such a short time before we got married, just twelve weeks or so.' Stupid. Very stupid. 'He was... different afterwards, but by the time I was beginning to think we'd made a mistake I found out I was expecting a baby. Two, as it happens.' She gave a wan smile but his dark face was still in the lengthening shadows. 'I'd had a stomach upset on honeymoon. They said it had probably interfered with the pill. Richard wanted me to have an abortion and we rowed terribly when I refused.'

She shifted slightly in her chair, wondering why she was telling this to Steel Landry, of all people. 'I'd always thought my going through with having the babies had made our marriage the way it was, blamed myself for it, I suppose, although I would never have considered doing anything else but what I did. Of course I knew nothing about the gambling, this whole other life he lived. Whether I could have helped him if I'd found out, I don't know.'

'Not if he didn't want to be helped,' Steel said quietly. 'The first step in conquering any form of addiction has to be a desire to be rid of it.'

She nodded. 'I suppose so.'

'I know so.' He hesitated for a moment. 'My father was an alcoholic, on and off the wagon once or twice a year. Most of the time he was a good husband and father, but when he was on a bender...' He shook his head. 'But my mother loved him. He'd been on the wagon for months before they went out one night with friends to celebrate their twentieth wedding anniversary. He started drinking that night and although he wasn't falling-over drunk when he left the pub he was on his way. Apparently, according to one of their friends, my mother wanted to drive but he wouldn't let her. He changed when he was drunk and she wasn't strong enough with him so she gave in. He killed himself and my mother and a young couple with a four-month-old baby in the crash that followed.'

'Steel...' Even in the darkness she sensed his pain.

'If my mother had phoned me I would have gone and picked them up, she knew that. I'd just bought my first old jalopy.' He stopped abruptly and she felt rather than saw him take control. When he next spoke his voice was flat, cool. 'He liked it too much to want to be rid of it, that was the thing. Just like your ex. When the need was there it didn't matter about anything or anyone. An addiction does that. It's evil.'

'I'm so sorry,' she whispered.

'It was a long time ago. I'm merely illustrating the truth that you couldn't have helped Richard unless he was willing.'

It might have been a long time ago but he was still hurting. Toni leant forward but the words she'd been about to say were never voiced. Instead her mother bustled out of the house, her father following with the tray of coffee, and the moment was lost.

It was only ten minutes or so later that her parents said they were going to bed and took their leave of Steel. 'We find it's early to bed and early to rise since the twins came,' Vivienne said with a smile. 'It's been a long time since Toni was small and I'd forgotten what energy little children have.'

Steel had stood up to shake their hands. Now he watched them go and resumed his seat as he said, 'I must let you get to bed too. I'll finish my coffee and make tracks, OK?'

Toni nodded but made no comment. It hadn't escaped her notice that for the last ten minutes or so Steel had concentrated on talking to her parents and had barely glanced her way. To all intents and purposes nothing had changed since he'd divulged the facts about his father, but she could sense a definite coolness where there'd been warmth before. It shouldn't matter but it did. He clearly regretted talking to her. Maybe he thought she would gossip? She wondered how she could reassure him without bringing up a subject he clearly didn't want to discuss any more.

Looking at her, Steel knew exactly what she was thinking. Her face was very expressive, the exact opposite of most of the cool, elegant, superbly controlled women he liked to date. *She* was the exact opposite. And therein lay his problem. He had no concerns she would discuss his father with anyone; it was more the fact he had found himself revealing what had happened that had panicked him. He'd never talked about the incident that had shattered his family and left himself and Annie orphans, not even to well-meaning family and friends, and certainly not to the lady from social services who had tried to press him to come to counselling at the time of the accident.

Somewhere in the distance a dog barked, the sound intruding into the sheltered little garden where only the low hum of distant traffic served as a background to the scented night. He drained his coffee cup and stood up, feeling the need to distance himself from her and take stock. For the first time in his life he felt as though his feet were on shifting sand and he didn't like that; he didn't like it at all. All the circumstances surrounding her were wrong and he'd known the moment he'd agreed to the mother's bidding to come into the house he was treading on dangerous ground, so why the hell had he done it? Why had he followed the desire to meet her family, her children, and why had he shamelessly played on the mother's soft heart to wangle a dinner invitation?

This wasn't like him. Dammit, he didn't *feel* like himself. He was autonomous and independent; he didn't do happy families in any shape or form. Everything in his life was on his terms and that was the way he liked it. And why the hell was he brooding over this right now anyway?

Toni had risen too, and as he walked round the little table she was saying something or other about how pleased she was she'd been to the site today and what a lot of ideas it had given her, but that was on the perimeter of his mind. He knew exactly what he was going to do. There could be no excuse afterwards about it being an impulse; he was going to kiss her because he wanted to. It was as simple as that. Simple, and hideously complicated.

His gaze fell to her mouth as he took her into his arms before she realised what he was doing. Her lips parted as she tried to speak, and he felt heat like liquid fire racing through his body as he took her mouth. She smelled as sweet as the night and was as warm, her hands resting against his chest as he let the kiss deepen slightly, shamelessly testing the water.

He had told himself that a kiss, a swift goodnight kiss at the end of an evening, could be explained away as social politeness, but now she was in his arms he knew he'd been fooling himself. He couldn't draw away. He deepened the kiss still more, his tongue rippling along her teeth until she opened fully for him, and as she kissed him back it sent his senses reeling.

Her hands had risen to his shoulders and now the delectable length of her body was pressed against his. As his fingers tangled in the raw silk of her hair she arched towards him with a little involuntary moan that destroyed the last of his shaky control. She was delicious, intoxicating.

He placed a hand in the small of her back to steady her as he plunged into the undefended territory of her mouth, fuelling and feeding on the fierce rush of sensation the feel and taste of her was producing in every inch of his body.

He wanted her, right now, on the stone slabs under the stars. He wanted to make love to her in this velvet darkness until there was no room in her mind for anyone or anything but him. He wanted to possess her completely, to make her his.

Her tongue had joined in the blistering exploration, stroking the rough inside of his mouth and provoking such heat he felt he was burning up, that only one thing would quench the agony. The kiss was now a kind of consummation in itself and his thighs were hard against hers, his heart pounding like a sledgehammer. He moved, pressing her against the wall of the house, but in the next moment his mobile phone began to ring, shrill and painfully persistent as it destroyed the magic.

He felt her freeze. He was breathing hard as he straightened away from her and he swore softly as his fingers fumbled for the phone, which he turned off without looking at it.

Toni had her hands to her cheeks and when she reached out blindly behind her, searching for the handle of the back door, he made no attempt to stop her as she turned and entered the house.

Steel stood for a moment, running a hand round the back of his neck and wondering what the hell had just happened. He was stunned by the raw desire that had hit him so suddenly and provoked such a powerful chain reaction. What had begun as a goodnight kiss had exploded into something outside his imagination; a seduction of mind, soul and body. But who, he asked himself, had been seducing whom?

And then he shook his head at himself, remembering the look on Toni's face when she had edged into the house. She had been mortified. Damn it all, how could he have been so stupid? She worked for him, for crying out loud, and he'd just broken every rule in the book.

Did she think he was in the habit of forcing himself upon the women who worked for him? He groaned softly, raking back his hair with a savage hand. Hell, what a mess. How could they work together after this? And she needed the job; there were the debts for a start, and if she was going to make a new life for herself and her girls it was imperative she earnt a good monthly salary. This place was far too small for them all now; as the twins grew it would get worse. Why hadn't he thought of this before he'd kissed her? She'd made it clear she didn't want a man around and what had he done? Bulldozed in like some callow youth who kept his brain in his trousers.

OK, OK, calm down. He breathed deeply, summoning the control that had always served him well in the past. When all was said and done he'd done no more than kiss her. It had been stupid and unprofessional but if he made it clear it wouldn't happen again this whole episode stood the chance of dying a natural death.

He knew what he was dealing with now. For some reason he couldn't fully trust himself around Toni and so he wouldn't put himself in such a position again. He'd treat her the same as his other employees and nothing more. From her side she'd been to hell and back the last few years and it was obvious she hadn't been on good terms with her husband for a long time. Tonight there'd been the moonlight and the wine and the euphoria of knowing she had the chance of getting her life back on some even footing again. He'd caught her at a vulnerable moment and she'd responded without thinking about it. It was just unfortunate that they were clearly sexually well matched.

The cold reasoning and logic were helping. Toni George was just an employee. An employee who was damn good at her job, admittedly, and for that reason he didn't want to lose her. That being the case, he had to make this all right, take all the blame and reassure her he wouldn't lay a finger on her in the future.

*Could he make that promise, though?*

The thought came out of nowhere and caused his mouth to set in a grim line. He'd have to. End of story.

Toni was waiting for him in the kitchen when Steel walked into the house. If she could have sunk through the floor and disappeared she would have done so; she had never felt so ashamed of herself in the whole of her life. He had kissed her—a 'thank you' for the meal and the evening—and what had she done? Practically eaten him. She clenched her teeth against the humiliating memory. He had been surprised, she knew he had, in the moment before he'd responded to her blatant invitation. And what man wouldn't? Lay it on a plate for any red-blooded single man—and some who weren't single, come to it—and they'd be up for it. It was the way men were made. Sex to them was like eating and drinking and as elemental as breathing, but without the emotional element necessary to most women.

She could hardly believe she'd reacted in such a way; it had never been like that with Richard or any of her boyfriends before him. Some of them had kissed well and some not so well, but Steel... Her traitorous senses were still tasting him, the feel of his mouth, warm and urgent against hers, his kiss hinting at pleasures and passion she'd never imagined in her wildest, most erotic dreams since she had met him.

She stared at him, utterly bereft and not knowing what to say or do, her cheeks burning hot and her hands icy cold.

'That was inexcusable,' he said quietly.

For an awful moment she thought he was talking about her behaviour and her heart stopped beating.

'I want you to know it won't happen again, Toni. You have my word. My only defence is that I didn't expect to lose control in that way, but once I held you in my arms...' He hesitated. 'Somehow a desire stronger and more compelling than I've ever known took over, but it's no excuse. Merely an explanation.'

'It—it wasn't your fault,' she stammered helplessly. 'I shouldn't have— I mean—'

'It was totally my fault.'

His voice was strained and she took a little comfort from it; she wouldn't have been able to bear it if he'd been blasé about the most devastating experience of her life. And it had been. She'd made love with Richard, she'd had his children and then tried to make the marriage work by being accommodating in bed and trying to please him, but never had she felt anything akin to the sweeping passion and desire that had taken her over tonight. And all he'd done was kiss her. What would it be like to make love with him? To spend a night of endless pleasure in his arms?

He was still standing just inside the doorway and his voice was low as he repeated, 'Totally my fault, I know that, but the bottom line is you have my assurance this won't be repeated. I don't want to lose you, Toni. You're a damn good interior designer and with the plans I have for the future you could go far. I'd hate to think that my stupidity would interfere with that. We will need to work closely together at various times; will you be able to do that after my assurance that this mistake was a one-off?'

*Mistake.* The word hit her between the eyes, producing a piercing shaft of pain before she told herself that of course that was what it had been. A mistake. One he regretted as much as she did. And that was fine. Just fine. Suddenly, for the first time since he had kissed her, anger was there. It provided a healthy dose of adrenaline that put iron in her backbone and acid on her tongue. 'Of course,' she said coolly, wishing she hadn't run from him outside like a scared rabbit. 'It was nothing, after all, just one of those things that happens sometimes when the atmosphere's right and one's had a glass or two of wine after a hard day's work.'

The silver eyes surveyed her steadily but a muscle jumped in his jaw, the only thing that indicated he hadn't liked her tone. 'Not to me, it doesn't, and I'd like you to know I don't make a habit of mixing work and play. This was a first.'

Did he expect her to be honoured? she thought waspily. She nodded tightly. 'It's already in the past.'

'Thank you.'

'I'll see you to the door,' she said quietly, her voice completely neutral and screamingly at odds with the turmoil inside.

She stood aside for him to pass her after she had opened the front door, vitally aware of every handsome muscled inch of him as he brushed past her and stepped down onto the pavement. He didn't immediately walk to the car, looking at her with glittering silver eyes for a moment. 'Thank your mother again for the meal, would you? You have a lovely family.'

Now she wanted to cry, which was unthinkable. Speech was beyond her so she moved her mouth in a smile as she nodded.

He studied her for a second more, the lean, strong face imperturbable. 'Goodnight, Toni,' he said, very softly, before turning away.

# CHAPTER SIX

'YOU COULD HAVE him for sexual harassment. From the sound of it he wouldn't miss a million or two and you need it more than he does. Hit him where it hurts, in his wallet.'

Toni stared at her best friend; she wasn't sure if Poppy was joking or not. Very happily married with three children under the age of five, Poppy was the typical earth mother: plump and rounded with a natural prettiness that owned nothing to cosmetics and all to good organic living. She also possessed a wicked sense of humour, which had been the thing that had drawn the two girls into a close friendship when they had met at antenatal classes. As luck would have it Poppy lived quite close to Toni's mother and Poppy's eldest child and the twins were due to start the same school in September. Poppy had already offered to help out, taking the twins to and from school any time Toni's mother couldn't, and although that wasn't necessary Toni appreciated the offer.

'I told you, he's been the perfect gentleman since Monday night,' Toni said weakly, 'besides which if there was any sexual harassment going on I think it was more me than him.' She glanced out of Poppy's kitchen window to where the twins were shrieking with delight as Poppy's eldest boy, a sturdy four-year-old with a voice like a foghorn, chased them with a small bucket of water. It was a baking hot weekend and Poppy had filled the paddling pool with tepid water after all the children had stripped down to their pants and been covered with suncream.

It had been a relief to talk the incident through with Poppy. She'd kept it to herself all week and the strain had been getting to her. Now she wondered if she'd done the right thing.

'So he's pretty drop-dead gorgeous, is he, this boss of yours?' Poppy leant forward, putting her elbows on the kitchen table where they were sitting having coffee and cake. 'Tell me all the sordid details.'

Toni smiled wryly. 'You ought to get out more.'

'Tell me about it.' Poppy patted her enormous stomach wherein her fourth child lay. Besides Nathan, the four-year-old, she had David, who was three, and little Rose, who would be a year old when the new baby made its appearance. They already knew it was another girl and Poppy had decided two of each was enough and Graham, her husband, was already scheduled for the snip.

'Seriously though,' Poppy continued, 'if you fancy him and he fancies you, what's wrong with a little fling? You're a free woman, Toni, and after the life you had with Richard a bit of rampant sex would be just the tonic you need.'

Toni eyed her friend severely. 'For one thing he doesn't particularly fancy me; I told you, it was more me than him.' The recollection of how she'd practically begged him to make love to her with that kiss was still too raw to talk about in any detail, and she went on hurriedly, 'Added to which I've only been a widow a matter of months and "rampant sex", as you put it, isn't my style with a virtual stranger.' Or anyone else, come to it. Poppy had been free with her favours before she met Graham and settled down and had hardly been able to believe it when Toni had told her Richard had been her first and only lover.

'He won't be a stranger the more you work with him,' Poppy said reasonably. 'Especially if your mother invites him to dinner.'

'He's my *boss*.'

'So? I had great rumpy-pumpy when I worked for that marketing executive. There's something about an office desk…'

'This is different,' said Toni, trying not to laugh.

'OK, we'll talk adult and grown-up. You kissed. No more, no less. Not exactly mind-blowing in the twenty-first century, Toni. And you let him know you enjoyed it. So what? That's a compliment to him, surely? Far better than gagging.'

Toni giggled; she couldn't help it. A few minutes with Poppy and she always felt better.

'He knew all about Richard and he'd met the girls, he realised you weren't in the running for a quick affair and so he did the decent thing and stepped back a mile or two. Respected you as a wife and mother. Well, ex-wife, but very much a mother. And now you can earn a shedload while working for a gorgeous piece of eye candy who won't try anything on and respects your saintly position. You've got everything you want. Stop feeling awkward, relax, and enjoy the job. You do enjoy it, don't you?'

'Love it.' Toni smiled and silently blessed Rose, who chose that moment to wake up from her morning nap. Time for a change of subject. She appreciated her friend's take on the situation and Poppy was probably right, but then she didn't have to work with Steel every day. Try as she might, and she knew it was completely unreasonable, it rankled that from Tuesday morning, when she had arrived at the office not knowing if she was on foot or horseback, Steel had been his smooth, unruffled, urbane self. Monday night could have been a dream, a fantasy, and there were a couple of times during that day when she'd had to reassure herself it *had* actually happened.

But it had. Oh, it had. And to her chagrin Steel had awakened something in her that evening that made it impossible for her to revert to the woman she had been before he'd kissed her. He'd inadvertently opened Pandora's box, which was monumentally unfair, leaving her—as it did—in the middle of nowhere. She didn't want Steel, or any other man, intruding into the safe, orderly world she had now, a world where she and the girls were impregnable.

In the last couple of years of her marriage she had never known how Richard would be when he walked through the door. Sometimes he was merely withdrawn, ignoring the twins and pushing her away when she tried to talk to him. Other times he'd been downright hostile and then she'd had to try and keep the girls out of his way completely. He had never gone so far as to be physically violent with Amelia and Daisy, but once or twice when he'd lost his temper over something they'd done or said she had felt he might be. The stress had been unbelievable. She would never put the girls in that position again. Never introduce a fourth person into their precious circle, someone with the potential to let them down. They were secure and in safe hands with her. That was all that mattered. They hadn't asked to be born and her wants and needs didn't count now.

The rest of the morning was spent running round after the children and talking of inconsequentials, but as Toni was leaving she was surprised when Poppy put her arms round her in a hug that was more than just a polite farewell. 'I know how awful it's been, really, I do, and you've still got all that debt and so on, but you're only thirty years old, Toni. There's someone out there for you, I know it. Someone who would be good to the girls too. Don't close your mind to that in the future.'

Toni hugged her back even as she thought, I don't want to hear this, Poppy. You know me but you don't know *me*, not over this. But then Poppy was blissfully happy with Graham and he worshipped the ground she walked on. Poppy had never experienced nights of lying awake wondering how she could face the next year, the next ten years, the next few decades with a man she had nothing in common with, and then finding out she'd only had a travesty of a marriage after all. And she was glad Poppy hadn't had to go through that, of course she was, but unless you had you didn't *know* how it was. Her marriage had been a tissue of lies from beginning to end; the only real thing in it all had been her beautiful girls. Men weren't to be trusted; she knew that now.

Amelia was uncharacteristically quiet on the way home. Toni felt her head but it wasn't hot and she didn't seem to be sickening for anything. All was revealed that evening as she tucked the girls up in bed, prior to reading their night-time story. Out of the blue, Amelia stated, 'Nathan said if you lose one daddy you can get another one. His friend Archy has had two already.'

Toni warned herself not to react. Very calmly, she said, 'We're all right as we are, aren't we? You like living with Grandma and Grandad and we all have lots of fun together.'

Amelia considered this. 'But it's not the same as having a daddy, is it? Nathan has got a daddy and *two* lots of grandmas and grandads.' This was said in the tone of 'it's not fair'.

'But I've explained to you that your daddy's mummy and daddy died before you were born.'

'They were very old,' Daisy put in importantly.

'Yes, that's right, sweetpea.' Toni hoped that would be the end of the conversation but, knowing her daughter, she doubted it.

Sure enough, Amelia wriggled a little before saying, 'Why couldn't we get another daddy, like the steel man? Me an' Daisy liked him. He was nice.'

'He's too busy to be a daddy.'

It was the wrong thing to say. She knew it even before Amelia piped up, 'Daddy was busy all the time but he was still Daddy. You can be a daddy *and* be busy, and we like the steel man, don't we, Daisy?'

Helplessly, Toni murmured, 'But you wouldn't want another daddy to be busy all the time, surely? If you ever have another daddy it would be nice to find one who can play with you and come on holiday with us, things like that, wouldn't it?' Richard had always insisted he was too tied up at work to holiday with them and she and the girls had gone away with her parents for a week in Cornwall each year.

Amelia wriggled some more. 'Suppose so,' she muttered reluctantly. 'But the steel man was nice.'

Toni smiled at the tiny power house who was her daughter and then turned to Daisy, who was watching her with huge brown eyes. 'It'll all work out, honeybee, don't worry,' she said softly. 'We've got each other and that's all that matters.'

Daisy beamed back and snuggled up against her, but Amelia slid under the covers without touching her mother. 'I'd still like a daddy,' she whispered, cuddling her teddy bear. 'A proper one, like Nathan's.'

Hiding her pain, Toni said briskly, 'Well, who knows what the future might bring, darling? But for now you've got to make do with just me and Daisy and Grandma and Grandad. How about we go on a picnic tomorrow and maybe in the afternoon we could visit that swimming pool you like, the one with the big slides and wave machine? We could see if Nathan and David want to come with us.'

'Yes, yes, yes!' Both girls bounced up and threw their arms round her neck.

Once the twins were asleep Toni sat watching them for a long time, her heart breaking. She had expected the sort of questions Amelia had put to her one day; just not so soon.

She rubbed tense neck muscles and walked over to gaze out of the window. In some of the other little gardens families were having barbecues or sitting enjoying the last of the sunshine together, and directly below the window her parents were reading over a cup of coffee at the patio table. As she watched them her father leant across and touched her mother's cheek. A simple gesture but one filled with love.

Jerking back into the room, Toni found she was fighting the tears, a poignant sadness gripping her. She had never felt so alone and lost and for a moment it seemed she was shrinking, disappearing into a little speck of nothing as she contemplated endless evenings like this one in the future.

And then one of the girls stirred in her sleep, muttering, 'Mummy,' before settling down again.

Toni walked across to look down at them and as she stood there her heart filled with thanksgiving for her babies. She had to count her blessings and the biggest two were right here, healthy and happy and safe. She was all at sixes and sevens at the moment, but was it any wonder with all that had happened in the last months? And she didn't know why she was feeling like this tonight; she had coped so well up to this point.

For a moment a dark male face was there on the screen of her mind, a pair of stunningly beautiful silver-blue eyes challenging the thought before she shook her head determinedly. No, it wasn't Steel Landry who had so unsettled her tonight. She wouldn't let it be. She worked for him, that was all, and she could dismiss the memory of what had happened that night in the garden just as easily as he apparently could.

Poppy was right. She'd fallen into a terrific job, which she absolutely loved, and she had got everything she wanted. She had to relax and go with the flow. Life was what you made it and she was going to make a good life for her and her daughters. It wasn't what she'd imagined in her teens—living life without a partner, a husband, someone to love and laugh and grow old with—but she had her girls and that was a lot more than some women had.

No more self-pity. She touched each of the girls' faces before leaving the room. She was back on track again.

This resolution was severely tested over the next weeks and months. Working with Steel proved to be exhilarating and stimulating and exhausting, but never, ever dull. Within the first month she could understand why once someone worked for him they rarely left unless they had to. Although a fiercely hardworking and exacting employer, he never asked one of his staff to do something he wouldn't do himself. In fact it was fair to say he worked harder and longer than anyone. And he was immensely generous when it came to holidays and time off and helping the families of those he employed. Bill's wife was by no means an isolated case. He actually seemed to *care* about his employees as people and not just efficient working machines. Although they definitely had to be that too. He simply didn't understand less than one hundred per cent commitment and loyalty.

Joy's replacement worked out well. Fiona was a very capable and friendly woman in her mid-forties who had been the breadwinner in her family most of her married life, due to her husband being diagnosed with multiple sclerosis when their two children were very young. Her boys were away at university now and the fact that they were twins provided an immediate bond between the two women.

Amelia and Daisy had sailed into big school life although Toni still received tales of the terrible Tyler most days, and as Toni paid for the girls to attend an after-school facility, where they were cared for until six o'clock when she picked them up, the load on her parents had lessened considerably.

So, everything in the garden was coming up roses, or it would have been but for the persistent and ridiculous feelings regarding Steel, which were a daily battle. Maybe if he hadn't kissed her that night, if he hadn't aroused all sorts of dormant sexual desires she had never been aware of, maybe then she would have been able to learn to disregard her magnetic boss as a man. But he *had* kissed her, breathing life into a side of her that had the power to shock and agitate her in the cold clear light of day. Some mornings she had difficulty looking him in the face.

If only he didn't have such a—such a *physical* effect on her, she thought early one cold morning at the beginning of December. It had been six months she'd worked with him now, but every time she caught sight of him in the morning her heart beat rapidly and her mouth went dry. And it didn't help that, the more she'd got to know him, the more she appreciated his dry, slightly wicked sense of humour, his ability to laugh at himself, his cynical but definitely amusing take on life.

Toni pushed her hair back from her forehead as she stood gazing out of the kitchen window into the tiny garden dusted with white from a heavy frost the night before. Spider webs on her mother's pots and bushes surrounding the patio glinted and sparkled in the weak morning sunlight, and a carpet of diamond dust coated the stone slabs.

She took a sip of the coffee she'd made for herself before the rest of the household awoke, and contemplated the day ahead. The apartments having been finished the week before and immediately snapped up, Steel now had a list of rich and influential would-be buyers for the new project that had been started while the apartments were still being worked on. This was the conversion of an enormous old riverside inn sitting in a quarter of an acre of ground into four three-bedroom apartments, complete with a new garage block over which was planned a caretaker's flat. The whole would be surrounded by an eight-foot brick wall and electric gates, with enough security to match Fort Knox.

But it wasn't the inn on the agenda today. Before she

had left the office the night before, Steel had told her
they'd be visiting a property outside London this morning, midway between the capital and Oxford. She had
nodded interestedly. 'Another conversion?'

'Not exactly, no. Just come and see the place with an
open mind anyway and then I'll tell you my plans for
it,' he'd said, somewhat cagily, Toni thought now.

They had been sitting in Steel's office at the time,
a routine they seemed to have slipped into before she
left to pick up the twins each evening. Initially the chat
and cup of coffee at the end of the working day had
been a time for discussing any problems or difficulties that had occurred on the job, but somewhere in the
time between June and December it had changed into
something more...

What, exactly? She frowned, her gaze caught by the
robin who appeared on the window sill outside, peering
in the window and reminding her she hadn't put his cake
out that morning. Delving into the cupboard for the cake
tin, she cut him a generous chunk of her mother's fruit
cake and opened the back door, crumbling his breakfast
on the sill in front of him. He didn't bother to move,
watching her as she retreated and pecking even as she
closed the door. He'd brought young ones along in the
summer but since they'd matured he'd seen to it they
were sent packing.

Her mind returned to Steel; she asked herself what
it was about their evening chats that was so unsettling.
Since the incident in the garden in the summer he'd been
propriety itself; she could have been a man for all the
impact she made on him. This thought wasn't new and
one she didn't like to dwell on. It had the power to ruin
her day.

Perhaps it was the fact that they now tended to discuss

anything and everything in a way she'd never had with anyone before. And he was more relaxed in the evenings and unfortunately ten times more attractive, often sitting with his tie loose and the first few buttons of his shirt undone revealing the beginnings of the black curly hair on his chest. She was galled just how much this affected her, especially in view of his indifference to her, but the flagrant masculinity was all the more potent for its naturalness. He was just one of those men who *radiated* maleness, she told herself irritably. Oozed it. Every little gesture, the way he held his head, the way he walked…

She finished her coffee, washing up her mug along with a couple of dishes from supper the night before. Her mother's tiny kitchen didn't boast a dishwasher.

She had a shower and got dressed before she woke the twins and took her parents their morning cup of tea in bed. By the time she dropped the twins off at school for their breakfast club a beautiful December day had unfolded, the sky high and blue and a winter's sun casting wisps of pale yellow light over the world below. It was good to be alive on such a morning.

Steel had obviously been working for some time when she arrived at the office and he called her into his room. His desk was strewn with papers, the biscuit tin was open and the delicious smell of coffee permeated the air. 'Don't take your coat off. We're leaving straight away,' he said, fastening the first couple of buttons of his shirt and pulling his tie into place as he spoke. 'And bring a notebook with you.'

'OK.' It was all she could manage, having caught the clean scent of his aftershave as he'd raked his fingers through his hair. It was a habit of his, the attempt to control the quiff of hair that was forever falling onto his forehead no matter how short he had his hair. She could imagine its refusal to obey irritated him no end. She didn't know how it had the temerity!

He also narrowed his eyes slightly and pulled at his left ear when he was considering something, became completely deadpan when he was unsure of his ground—which wasn't often—and had a delicious way of quirking his mouth when something had struck him funny when it shouldn't have.

Oh, she knew quite a bit about what made her one-in-a-million boss tick, Toni thought wryly. Apart from his love life. In all their discussions he'd never mentioned women, for which she was eternally grateful. And the office grapevine had gone silent on the subject too. Normally, apparently, Steel's latest woman was discussed and dissected at length. The last one to be mentioned—a flame-haired attorney with a body to die for, according to most of the men—had bit the dust months and months ago. Rumour had it that Barbara Gonzalo had been as passionate and vibrant as her name suggested, but she'd committed the cardinal sin of falling in love with him. She had been very vocal when he'd finished their relationship, even going so far as to storm into the office the morning after and cause a scene that had rocked the building. Toni could just imagine how that had gone down with Steel.

They left the office and entered the lift, and once it had deposited them in Reception he took her elbow as they crossed the foyer. Immediately a heated weakness suffused her body. It was always the same. His slightest touch seemed to set off a chain reaction in her body she was powerless to do anything about.

They were in the Aston Martin and on their way

before he said, 'This project is slightly different from the others, Toni.'

Glad he was speaking at last—he'd been silent and withdrawn so far—she nodded in what she hoped was an efficient way. 'Oh, yes?' she asked encouragingly.

'I'm thinking of buying a house, somewhere I can escape to but which is still not too far from London.'

Completely taken aback, she stared at the expression-less profile. 'Oh.' Not exactly an intelligent comment, a separate part of her brain noted. Bringing her mind to bear, she said, 'And you want me to suggest ideas if you decide it's what you want? Throw a few facts and figures into the equation?'

'Exactly. You're a woman—'

So he *had* noticed, Toni thought sourly. How kind.

'And you'll provide a different viewpoint as well as a creative slant. It'll need plenty doing to it if I buy it.'

She nodded again. 'I see.' She thought of his apart-ment—ultra-modern and gadget-mad with enough stain-less steel and neutrality to satisfy any self-respecting bachelor—and knew she wasn't going to like this house. She didn't fool herself that when he spoke of 'escaping' it would be by himself, and everything in her baulked at the idea of contributing to a love nest for Steel and his entourage of women. Stifling her emotion, she said quietly, 'Have you seen the property before?'

'Had a look at it a few days back.'

Had he been alone then or with someone? Just be-cause the gossip mongers hadn't got hold of his latest partner it didn't mean he was currently single. Why would he be?

Once they had left the city behind the road snaked past barren white fields, the grizzled countryside they were beginning to travel past stark and bare but holding a desolate beauty nonetheless. Toni relaxed a little. She loved the country. Both her mother's and father's parents had lived deep in Hertfordshire, which was where her parents had grown up and met, and she could recall wonderful summer holidays at their respective homes when she'd been as free as a bird to run wild from morning till night. Real log fires; cottage gardens ablaze with all the old-fashioned flowers like hollyhocks and lupins and sweet peas and a beautifully tended vegetable patch; warm, fresh brown eggs for breakfast from her grandparents' much-loved and cosseted hens, and listening to the owl hooting outside the house when she was snug in bed—it had been a magical time. She had been truly happy then, before the world and its ways had thrust her into a harsher awareness of life.

They passed a couple of towns and villages and had been travelling for quite a while before Steel murmured, 'Not much further now. The house is set by itself just outside a village, but a large market town is only ten miles away so it's not too remote a location.'

Toni nodded but didn't comment. The journey had been conducted in almost total silence and, for some reason she couldn't explain, she was feeling nervous. It wasn't only that she was alone with Steel, although that always caused an agitated trembling deep inside, but he seemed different this morning somehow. Over the last months, working so closely together on his pet projects, she'd thought she had seen all his moods, but this was a new one. The man had more guises than a chameleon.

'What's the matter?' he asked suddenly, pulling off the main road and into a long country lane guarded by sentinel-like trees either side of the high hedgerow.

'The matter?' She glanced quickly at him but he was

concentrating on a bend in the lane and the hard profile gave nothing away. 'I don't know what you mean.'

'You were frowning.' He smiled. 'Quite distinctly.'

'Was I?' she asked in genuine surprise.

'What were you thinking?' he asked softly.

She knew him well enough by now to know he would persist until he got an answer, and he always seemed to be able to detect a lie. Keeping her voice steady, she said, 'I was just thinking you don't seem yourself this morning, that's all.'

He shot her a look of sardonic amusement. 'Is that so?' he drawled lazily. 'And what, exactly, is myself?'

'I'm sorry?' She wished she hadn't spoken now.

'How would you sum me up, Toni?'

This conversation wasn't going at all as she wanted. There had been one or two other occasions lately when he'd displayed a somewhat mordant slant, but they'd been short-lived and gone in minutes. Impossible man.

'Ah, I see you consider that too personal a question. Am I right? All the little shutters have gone up with a vengeance.'

She'd often got the feeling he was laughing at her and this was one of those times. Annoyance brought an edge to her voice as she said, 'You might consider my reply too personal if I answered truthfully.' And put that in your pipe and smoke it.

'Touché.' He grinned that sexy, charming grin of his and her heart began an undignified gallop. 'So do I take it I haven't managed to redeem myself over the last six months?'

Was he *flirting* with her? He couldn't be. Not Steel. Toni found she wanted to put a hand to her chest to still her hammering heart but didn't dare to. Instead she forced herself to speak calmly and steadily: 'I don't know what you mean.'

'Do you know you always say that when you're pre-varicating?' His tone wasn't critical, more casually amused with a warm edge to it. 'And you rub your nose when you're enthusiastic about something and hold onto your bottom lip with your teeth when you're listening intently.'

She stared at him, unable to say a word or spring back with one of the witty responses she was sure his girlfriends would use. He'd been observing her while she'd been observing him?

'And there's a note in your voice when you talk about your children that's never there at any other time.' He drew the car to a stop and cut the engine. 'Here we are,' he continued, as offhandedly as though they'd just been discussing the weather. 'I'll just open the gates. They're supposed to be automatic but they don't work; one of many things which will need attending to if I take the house.'

He slid out of the Aston Martin and opened the mas-sive wrought-iron gates set in a high red-brick wall. Toni watched him, her head whirling.

Once he'd climbed back in the car he drove on to a long winding drive bordered on each side by lawns, shrubs and trees. The house was a hundred yards or so in front of them, a mellow old building with honey-coloured stone and a thatched roof. It was as different from what she'd expected as could possibly be.

Her face must have expressed her thoughts because beside her Steel murmured, 'Surprised? What did you have me down for? No, let me guess. A new build per-haps. Or maybe a barn conversion. Something with a modern feel anyway and perhaps a little soulless. Am I right?'

He was absolutely spot on. 'Not at all,' she said tightly, glaring at him. 'I had no thoughts about what to expect one way or the other.'

'Liar.' He left the car before she could retort, walking round the bonnet and helping her out of the low sleek vehicle with a solicitous hand at her elbow.

It was the tranquillity of her surroundings that hit Toni immediately, that and the sound of birdsong in the trees. She breathed in the crisp frosty air that smelt different from the fuel-laden fumes of the city and then gazed up at the house. It was beautiful, stunning, the quintessence of old-world charm. England at its best. She swallowed hard. 'How old is it?'

'Sixteenth century. At least the original part of the house is, but it's been extended. It sits in two acres and has magnificent views at the back. It even has its own small wood with resident badgers.' He smiled at her rapt expression. 'You like it, then? It meets with your artistic approval?'

'Who wouldn't like it? It's wonderful.'

'Reserve your opinion until you've seen inside. The setting is perfect but the house itself needs some work doing to it. The kitchen's small and outdated and the house itself is tired. I've got some ideas but I'd like your take on it.'

Toni nodded. She didn't care what the inside was like; this house was the sort of place dreams were made of.

Once inside she could see what Steel meant, but she could also envisage the house as it could be if it was sympathetically restored and the layout reworked a little. Downstairs there were a number of rooms but the kitchen was indeed very small. Upstairs there were eight good-size bedrooms but only one bathroom. It was clear nothing had been done to the house for decades. The view from the ground at the back of the property was breathtaking. She hadn't realised they were on a hill, but the lawns and flowerbeds and mature bushes and trees gently sloped down to the wood Steel had spoken of, and beyond that was rolling countryside for miles and miles.

'Spectacular, eh?'

They were standing outside the French doors leading from the main reception room on a patio that had seen better days. The blue sky above, the white sparkling world beneath and, not least, Steel standing so close she was vitally aware of the height and breadth and faint delicious smell emanating from the big frame caused her voice to wobble slightly as she said, 'Utterly.'

'So, can you see me here, Toni?' His voice was level, almost flat, and he didn't look at her as he spoke, keeping his eyes on the countryside spread out in front of them like an enormous beautiful picture.

She didn't reply immediately, considering exactly what to say. 'Yes,' she said at last, 'but—'

'But?' He gazed at her with hooded eyes. 'Always a *but*.'

'This is an enormous house for just one person. Wouldn't it be better to consider either a smaller property or an apartment somewhere outside the city, if that's what you want?'

He didn't reply to this. 'But you think I could suit this house?'

It was a strange way to put it. Normally one would ask if the house could suit them, but in this case he was absolutely right, Toni thought. This house was so special and so beautiful it shouldn't have to fit in with anyone—the boot had to be on the other foot. And the fact he'd put it that way made her voice firm when she said, 'Yes, I do. You've fallen in love with it, haven't you?'

He was very still for a moment. 'I've never been in love before but, yes, I think I am.'

Toni nodded. 'Then all the work and changes will be worth it. You must go with your heart for once.'

'My thoughts exactly.' Steel's silver-blue gaze followed a magpie that had just swooped over the trees onto the lawn carrying a morsel of something or other in its beak, which it now proceeded to eat. Six months and this woman had turned his life upside down and she was completely unaware of it. It had taken him weeks, probably a couple of months to adjust to the knowledge that Toni George was different.

Women abounded in London; beautiful, available and willing women, and he'd had his share until the day she had walked into his apartment and he'd looked into her eyes. Strange, but he couldn't put his finger on what made her special. She was very lovely, intelligent and gutsy, but those attributes could be laid at the feet of several women he knew. Women who carried no baggage and who definitely didn't have four-year-old twins in tow.

He'd sent the little girls a present each on their birthday—which he knew had taken Toni aback—and received in return two handmade cards of people with sticks for arms and legs and two scrawls at the bottom of the cards that were apparently their names. After that he had tried to take a big step backwards but it hadn't worked; nothing had. The more he'd got to know her, the more he had wanted her, which was a first for him. Normally he slept with a woman and then got to know her, which finished with him not wanting her. And now he was faced with the prospect of loving someone who certainly didn't love him back and who had no intention of letting a man into her life or anywhere near her family.

Steel smiled to himself. How many of his exes would take secret satisfaction in his predicament? The love-'em-and-leave-'em Steel Landry hoisted by his own petard. But he was damned if he was going to roll over and accept the situation. She'd responded to him sexually that night in June, which was a start, and she'd wanted him as much as he'd wanted her. He could make her love him. He'd been patient for months now, preparing the ground; this was the next stage. And to hell with the rule that he didn't mix work and pleasure. Being the boss had to mean something and in this case it was that rules were breakable.

One of the things that had amazed him about her was the lack of bitterness about her former husband. In spite of the way he'd treated her, she didn't hate the louse. True, it had made her wary and suspicious of the opposite sex, but that was to his advantage in a way. It kept the other wolves at bay.

He glanced down at her now, reaching out a hand and brushing a strand of hair from the silky skin of her cheek. He heard her quickly indrawn breath and his heart thumped crazily. Yes, she was far from indifferent to him as a man, but he didn't want to just take this woman to bed. He wanted *her*. 'Let's go and get some lunch and you can tell me some of the ideas I know are already buzzing about in that clever little head of yours,' he said smoothly. 'I noticed a nice pub shortly before we turned off into this side road, which is called

Magpie Lane, incidentally. Appropriate address for a family house, don't you think?'

It was a moment before she shrugged. 'Magpies are quite vicious birds, aren't they? Part of the crow family, I believe.'

'They do what's necessary to get by. Same as the rest of us. All's fair in love and war.'

'That's such a male reply,' she said stiffly.

'But I am a male, Toni, and don't tell me you haven't noticed, an observant, intelligent woman like you. I'm very much a male and I make no apology for it.' He opened the French doors as he spoke and when she stepped past him into the house he heard a muffled 'Huh', which made the corners of his mouth twitch. He had no illusions winning her over was going to be easy; she was as prickly as a cactus with as many spikes for keeping him at bay, but he was going to strip those little spines away one by one until he got what he wanted, which was her, naked and pliant in his arms and wholly his, soul, mind and body.

# CHAPTER SEVEN

THE PUB WAS ALL BRASSES and oak beams. Toni was not unaware of the little stir Steel caused in the two buxom barmaids, or the way they practically fought to serve him when he went to order drinks once they'd found a table close to the roaring log fire. He came back with a glass of wine for her and an apple juice for himself and two menus, sitting down and smiling at her as he murmured, 'I've surprised you today, haven't I?'

She eyed him warily. 'A little, I suppose.'

'Another surprise. I've decided we'll take the day off.'

*'What?'* She sat up straighter. 'What on earth for?'

'It's not often I decide to buy a house. I want to celebrate.' His smile widened, a little like a shark's. 'Besides which, I want to get a few facts and figures clear in my head before I make an offer. If I got into the office there's too much distraction.'

He saw her expression relax slightly. 'Oh, I see. You mean we'll still be working but on the ideas for this house.'

'If you want to put it like that.'

Her brows came together for an instant and she took a sip of wine. 'Steel—'

'Decide what you want to eat so we can order and

then you can tell me your plans for each room.' He picked up his own menu and pretended to be absorbed in it, only raising his head when one of the barmaids came across with a pad and pencil to take their order, practically drooling as she looked at Steel.

The meal decided, he met her gaze. 'So? Tell me your thoughts thus far.' The flames from the crackling fire in the big old hearth were picking out the red tints in her dark brown hair, her pale creamy skin and red lips a delicious contrast. Before she could speak, he murmured, 'Rose Red. From the fairy tale, you know? Has anyone ever told you that you look like Rose Red?'

She stared at him for a moment. 'The first thing to be tackled is the kitchen. It's too small and hopelessly outdated. I suggest you knock through into the old scullery and also the room next door, which is currently a breakfast room. That would give you a huge space to play around with, and if you go for Shaker-style units with pretty handles and granite worktops, and perhaps natural slate tiles on the floor, they'll fit in with the beamed ceiling and feel to the property. There'll be ample space for a kitchen table and chairs and so on.'

Steel nodded. 'Go on.'

'Apart from the original sitting room, which is quite wonderful as it is, there seems to be several small rooms downstairs as a result of the extension done to the original building. You don't need a morning room and a snug, not when you have a dining room and study and second sitting room already. If you sacrifice the morning room to extend the entrance hall to make more space as you come into the house, the snug could be changed into a downstairs cloakroom.' She paused for breath.

'Could all that be done without ruining the original features?' Steel asked thoughtfully.

Toni nodded, her face animated as it always was when she was starting a new project. 'Absolutely, and I know of a wonderful reclamation yard as well as a supplier of beautiful limestone that would look just right in the entrance hall. Upstairs if you sacrificed two of the bedrooms and divided each into two bathrooms, four bedrooms could have an en-suite. I'll draw that up for you later. And the master bedroom is more than big enough to incorporate an en-suite as it is. That would just leave the one bedroom next to the present bathroom and it would be easy to knock through. This would mean six bedrooms all with en-suites, which I think is preferable to eight without.'

'I agree.' He smiled. 'I was right to bring you.'

'The main sitting room, or drawing room I suppose, would be more imposing if four-panel doors were used to create a double-width entrance, but that's just a suggestion. It's fine as it is. But overall I think you need to be careful to create a look that's easy and timeless, something opulent and in keeping with the period feel but not heavy or dark. The mullioned windows are beautiful but they don't let in as much light as modern ones, so we need to concentrate on pale fabrics—creams and duck-egg blue and ochre for example—and do away with all those dark, patterned carpets. There are wonderful floorboards underneath them—I've checked. They'd only need to be sanded and sealed, and rather than hide them you could enhance them with rugs. Thick, luxurious ones in light shades.'

She came up for air to find Steel smiling at her.

'What?' she asked warily. Why was he looking at her like that?

'Sounds great. You're in charge.'

'In charge?' she echoed faintly. The way he'd said it…

'From start to finish and down to the last teaspoon in my new kitchen. Run with it. Forget the other projects. I can get those sorted. I want you to concentrate on this from now on. I only want to know if there's a problem. Otherwise, you have a free hand on the alterations, colours, fabrics, everything. And I don't want to see it until it's finished, OK?'

Her face registered alarm. 'Steel, this is your home we're talking about. You'll have to choose the kitchen you want and so on. I couldn't possibly presume to speak for you; you might hate my taste.'

'No.' He grinned at her, but for once she was too wound up to notice. 'I trust you implicitly.'

'It's not a question of *trust*. It's a matter of taste.'

'But you have perfect taste, Toni,' he said solemnly.

'You know what I mean. It's not like these are apartments or something. I couldn't take over completely.'

'You can't do your job?' He raised one eyebrow.

'This is not my job,' she protested adamantly.

'You are employed by me as an interior designer and I've asked you to be in sole charge of a job from beginning to end. It's as simple as that. I have no experience in creating a family home, which is what I'm wanting here; furthermore I'd find the details tiresome. You have free rein with the financial side and money is not a problem.'

'But you must see that the house will be as I'd like it, which isn't necessarily how you'd feel comfortable. I shall need to consult you on furniture and fittings at least.'

'No.' He settled back in his chair, his eyes bright silver as he gave a small laugh, low in his throat. 'And forget what the apartment in London looks like. I want a change, OK? Like I said, this house is essentially a family home—you can feel it in the very brickwork. Obviously I'm not a family man but that's of no matter. When people walk through the front door I want them to feel a woman's touch in the place, something warm and welcoming. My sister and her husband will visit often; I want their child to feel completely at home here.'

Toni grabbed at his last words for normality; she was feeling knocked sideways by the responsibility of what he was suggesting. 'How is Annie?' she asked weakly. 'The baby must be due any time.' Cowardly to change the subject, she knew, but she'd come back to his amazing declaration when she'd had time to think about it.

'As we speak,' he agreed. 'Far from coming early, it now seems to want to remain where it is. She was due a couple of days ago but the doctors are satisfied all is well.'

'At least it's given them a chance to get everything ready.' Annie and her husband hadn't wanted to know the sex of the baby and so Jeff had arranged for the room they'd designated as a nursery to be painted in a pale lemon, according to Steel, who had insisted on buying all the baby furniture and equipment as his present to his nephew or niece.

Their meal came in the next moment but, although her steak pie was delicious, Toni found she'd lost her appetite. Steel had well and truly stepped out of his box this time and it disturbed her. He always disturbed her, but this time it was different.

A family home. She worried at the thought as she ate, like a dog with a bone. *Was* there someone in his life he'd kept hidden from gossiping tongues? A woman he perhaps felt he could settle down with? Someone special? And she'd have to be special to keep Steel. Someone very sure of herself, the way women constantly threw themselves at him, with a wit and intelligence to match his. Beautiful and confident enough to deal with any women determined to oust her from his affections, and strong enough to cope if the worst happened and he grew tired of her. A wonder woman, in fact.

She chewed slowly, the steak tasting like sawdust in her mouth. And why was she so upset at the notion of Steel with another woman? She would never want to be with someone like him in a month of Sundays.

The thought carried no weight, simply reminding her of her inadequacies. She was ordinary and always had been; he must have always been extraordinary to get to where he was now, and it would need a woman of the same ilk to hold him.

She found her insides were trembling. *From the prospect of renovating and overseeing the job of making his house into a warm, inviting family home?* No. *From imagining Steel living there with the woman who had captured his heart?* Maybe. Almost certainly. Which made her the biggest idiot in the world.

She pushed her plate away, the meal half eaten, and made the excuse she'd had a big breakfast as Steel raised his eyebrows and asked if she'd like something else.

As he shamelessly reached for her plate and deposited the contents on his own, she watched him as he tucked into the food with every appearance of enjoyment. What was it to her if he had met someone or did meet someone in the future? And why was she thinking like this today?

One of the barmaids appeared at his elbow, ostensibly to ask if they'd like more drinks, but as Toni watched the young girl flutter her eyelids at Steel she noted none of the other diners got such good treatment. The barmaid's blatant come-on confirmed everything Toni had been thinking and surprisingly steadied her. It was an answer to a question her mind wouldn't let her formulate.

She managed her treacle pudding and custard, and, when Steel's eyebrows rose again, smiled, before she said, 'I'm a dessert girl. I always have been.'

'Annie's the same. It used to be a battle to get her to eat her meat and veg if she knew a nice pudding was waiting.'

'You always speak of Annie as though she was your daughter rather than your sister.' It was out before she had thought and when she realised how personal it sounded she blushed a bright pink. He had no need to explain anything to her.

Steel didn't seem to notice. Quietly, he said, 'I guess that's true in a way. I brought Annie up after our parents died and I've always felt responsible for her.'

'That must have been hard at times when you were younger, before she met her husband.' Part of her couldn't believe she had the temerity to delve like this; the other part desperately wanted to know what he would say. 'Didn't you feel tied down?'

He looked down at the glass in his hand, clearly thinking about what she had said. His black lashes were thick and long for a man, thought Toni, but they only added to his masculinity somehow. A touch of softness emphasising the hardness.

'At the time I think I just got on with it,' he said after a moment or two. 'And I did still manage to have girlfriends. I wouldn't want you to run away with the impression I was a monk or anything. But after she met Jeff I have to admit I felt a weight had been lifted off me. Not that I didn't love her and want to take care of her,' he added quickly, 'and no one forced me to do it. There were other members of the wider family who would have taken her off my hands but I didn't want that. And I've never regretted those years. Not once.'

But they'd taken their toll. She realised he was letting her see a part of him that few people—if any—saw, and her heart swelled with an indescribable feeling before she took check of herself. This was still Steel Landry, she cautioned. Bachelor extraordinaire and magnet to any woman who set eyes on him. Keeping her voice even and bland, she said, 'Which is why you value your freedom now, of course.'

'Why I have done in the past, yes.'

Her breath stopped. He *did* have a woman, someone so precious he'd kept her from public gaze. That was what this 'family' house was all about. The knife-like pain that shot through her made her stomach muscles clench.

The waitress popped up again like a genie out of a bottle with their coffee, and in spite of the girl's gooey glances at Steel Toni silently blessed her for the much-needed moments to pull herself together. As the waitress sashayed off Toni took refuge in the mundane. 'They must be really excited now the time is so close when they'll see their first child.'

'I guess so.' He nodded slowly.

'Have they decided on names yet?' she asked woodenly.

'Names?' he echoed abstractedly, his eyes on her face.

'Annie and Jeff? For the baby?' She couldn't blame him for his blank expression. One minute they'd been talking nitty-gritty 'feeling' stuff, and the next...

He didn't bat an eyelid. 'Charles for a boy, Eve for a girl, at the last count, but it changes with the wind.

We've had every name beginning from A to Z; Annie's had too much time to think.'

'Poor Annie. The last few months have been difficult for her.'

'Poor Jeff. This weepy thing women go through in pregnancy has thrown him for six. He can cope with concepts that blow the normal human mind and technology that would have floored Einstein as easy as pie, but Annie crying sends him into a spin.'

'That's because he loves her,' Toni said quietly.

'Yes, he does.' Steel gave a crooked smile. 'He loves her very much.'

There *was* someone. She knew it. Toni took a gulp of her coffee and scalded the back of her throat. He was so different today, so not the Steel of office hours. And this was the man all his girlfriends saw; someone infinitely more devastating than even the powerful, ruthless tycoon she had become accustomed to. No wonder his women became obsessed with keeping him, as the unfortunate Barbara had done. How would you get over someone like Steel? Or perhaps you never did.

Suddenly she felt she was in one of those dreams where she knew it was imperative to escape the unseen threat bearing down on her but only to find her legs were like lead and she was unable to run. She blinked, taking a deep breath, and the panic receded, leaving her slightly shaky.

'More coffee?' Steel said softly. 'Or a brandy?'

'No. No, thanks.' She met his eyes, hers veiled. 'I really do need to get back to the office, Steel. There are several things I have to deal with today.'

He nodded, standing up and reaching for her coat on the back of her chair. As he helped her into it she was conscious of a feeling of disappointment at his easy capitulation and chided herself for her inconsistency. She really had to pull herself together, she told herself with uncomfortable truth. She was acting like a naive schoolgirl rather than a mature woman with two small children.

It was bitterly cold outside; the frost had barely dissipated at all and where the sun hadn't reached the ground it was as slippy as walking on glass. As her feet slid from under her Steel's arms shot out and caught her before she could fall, the momentum bringing her hard against his chest.

*She wanted him to kiss her more than she had ever wanted anything in her life.* The knowledge was there as she stared wordlessly up at him, and then he bent his head and fulfilled the longing that had burnt her up for six long months. He kissed her thoroughly and with an enjoyment he made no effort to hide.

His lips were cool and firm and tasted of the mints the waitress had brought with their coffee, and when his tongue swept inside the sweet honey of her mouth her senses went haywire. He withdrew after a few moments, only to begin the invasion anew and this time his head tilted to give his searching mouth full access. The kiss was everything she remembered and more.

Toni found herself arching towards him with a wantonness that would have horrified her only minutes before. Her lips moved instinctively, trying to deepen a kiss that was already immeasurable, and she clung onto him as though she were drowning.

One of his hands moved at the back of her neck and the next moment her hair was loose, cascading about her face as he threaded his fingers through it, supporting her head as he continued to explore her. His other arm was round her waist and she was moulded into the bulk of him, gloriously close.

She didn't think about anything but the feel and taste of him; he'd obliterated the past and future and the present was purely sensation. She was conscious of thinking that she didn't want the kiss to end, that she wanted to stay like this for ever, wrapped in his arms in the frosty air.

But, of course, it had to end. He raised his head slowly but didn't let go of her, wrapping his open overcoat round her so she was enfolded even more closely into him. 'Wow,' he breathed softly.

Her thoughts exactly. She blushed, still lost in the grip of sensual desire, but as the door to the pub opened and she heard voices she pulled slightly away, suddenly shy.

Steel smiled, putting his arm around her and keeping it there as they walked to the car. They didn't say a word, but once inside the Aston Martin's leather-clad interior he turned toward her and kissed her again, a light kiss, brushing her lips with his own. 'I've waited six months to taste you again. I'm not going to wait another six months,' he growled huskily. 'In fact six minutes would be pushing it.'

'Steel, this isn't right.' Somehow she found her voice. 'I can't do this.'

'Yes, you can.' He refused to accept her self-denial. 'Look how easy it is.' The third kiss was scorching, as he'd meant it to be, and she felt the impact right down to her toes.

Feeling trapped—whether by him or the strength of her reaction to him, Toni wasn't sure—she struggled away from him, leaning against the passenger door as she gasped, 'You don't understand.'

'Oh, I do, Toni. I do. Believe me, if I didn't understand I wouldn't have waited six months. But no more.
You can't deny there's something between us. I don't
know if you're ready to hear this now, but I'm going to
tell you anyway. I want you. You turn me on with your
velvet-soft eyes and silky skin and gentle ways; in fact
you send me crazy.'

She stared at him, hardly able to believe what she was
hearing. This couldn't be her he was talking about.

'I want to make love to you; I spend most of the
day thinking about it and then when I go to sleep it's
worse. The things we indulge in at night, Toni...' He
leant slightly closer, not touching her with any part of
himself yet enveloping her in his body warmth. 'It's
driven me insane playing the boss when I want to be
much, much more to you.'

'I'm—I'm not what you want,' she whispered.

Steel expelled a quiet breath. 'Yes, you are.' He
reached out and touched her lips with his finger. 'From
the moment I set eyes on you, in fact.'

'That's—that's just lust, sexual attraction.' She let
her hair fall forward, hiding her expression. 'You didn't
even know me then.'

'But I know you now. I know so much about you
now, and you know plenty about me too. What have
the last six months meant to you, Toni? All those chats
late at night when everyone else has gone? Did you look
forward to them? Enjoy finding out little things about
me?'

She wanted to sag against the car door as his words hit
home. It was only in this moment of blinding truth that
she realised she'd lived for those times with a strange,
intense excitement that had no rhyme or reason. 'You
did that on purpose?' she whispered helplessly.

His smile this time was merely a twitch. 'I scared the hell out of you six months ago and I didn't want that to happen again. You didn't trust me, maybe you still don't trust me, but we've moved forwards quite a way since then. Not enough—' this time his smile was self-deprecating '—not when I want to know you inside out; how you think and feel about everything, especially me. And I'm not talking about your sexual desire here. I know you have the taste of me and want more from the way you respond when I so much as touch you. But that apart, how do you see me? I asked you that once before and you didn't answer me. Why was that, I wonder?'

She shook her head, unable to reply.

'Don't shut me out, Toni. I want you and you want me and what we have is too powerful to fight.'

Her head jerked slightly as she drew in a steadying breath. He was talking about sex. In everything he'd said he'd only mentioned *wanting* her, nothing more. No talk of commitment or for ever or...love. And why would he? She knew that wasn't on Steel's agenda.

'I don't intend to rush you, in spite of how I've behaved today,' he said very calmly as she continued to remain silent. 'But however slow we take it, you and I are going to progress. That is set in concrete.'

'Steel, it takes two to agree something like that,' she said a little more strongly. He was taking a lot on himself!

'Four, in this case. I'm aware of that too.'

Four? And then she realised he was talking about Amelia and Daisy. To her mortification she became aware that in the last heady, intoxicating few minutes her precious girls hadn't featured in her thoughts. It had been all about her and Steel. Frankly horrified at herself, she lifted her eyes to his. 'I told you once before

I have no intention of introducing the twins to a series of "uncles".'

'And I told *you* then I was pleased to hear it. I still am. I don't intend for there to be a line, Toni. Amelia and Daisy know you work for me and they are bright little girls. They'll accept me in their life as a friend of yours.'

'A friend?' It would be funny if it weren't so serious.

'Exactly.' He smiled. 'Until you are ready for something more. I want you but I don't want to hurt you or cause you to feel threatened or have regrets because you feel I've seduced you into my bed. And I could do that so easily. We both know that.'

The male arrogance was too much. She glared at him. 'Really?' she said with scathing sarcasm. 'You're irresistible, is that it?'

Steel moved half into her seat, lowering his head and taking her mouth. He savoured the shape of her lips, the sweet taste of her, and after a token struggle he felt her mouth open beneath his probing. Within moments she was there with him every inch of the way as he deepened the kiss with the intent of showing her exactly what he wanted to be doing to her at that moment. He finished the embrace with a row of nibbling kisses along her jawline, stopping at the corner of her lips, and by then her breathing was raspy and her cheeks flushed with passion. OK, so he'd proved his point.

A wry smile curved his lips as he moved back fully into his seat, but the glitter in his silver eyes was a great deal more elemental. 'And that's without really trying. When I have you naked and willing in my arms it will be long and slow and lasting and we'll go to heaven and back. I can promise you that, my passionate little puritan.'

Toni stared at him helplessly. Logic told her it would be the biggest mistake of her life to let this carry on. She was already emotionally involved with this man and she still didn't know how it had happened, but if they became lovers she would never recover from the fallout when it finished. Lovers... It was the culmination of all her secret fantasies over the last months, all the long hours when she'd tossed and turned in her chaste little bed in an agony of need.

And then he took the decision out of her hands. 'I'm not going to take no for an answer, Toni,' he warned very softly. 'From employer and employee, we've now moved to friends, OK? And the next step's timing will be up to you.'

She stared at him, her eyes still dark with desire. 'Friends don't kiss, not like we have. Is this friendship going to be on more...platonic grounds?'

'Not a hope in hell, sweetheart.'

# CHAPTER EIGHT

It had gone far better than he'd expected. Steel glanced at Toni as they drove back to the city later that night. They had gone for a drive after their heart-to-heart in the car park, exploring the surrounding area for some thirty miles or so around the house before stopping for dinner at an imposing country hotel. Toni had telephoned her parents before they had left the pub after lunch and arranged for her mother to pick the twins up, and, although she hadn't exactly relaxed during the afternoon, she hadn't been distant or withdrawn. During dinner he'd set out to make her laugh and he'd succeeded. Yes, all in all it could have been a lot worse.

He glanced at her again as the car was forced to stop at traffic lights. She was sleeping, her hair forming a soft and silky veil and hiding her face from him. Even in her sleep she managed to elude him, he thought wryly. But no more. He refused to stay on the perimeter of her life for one more day, one more hour, one more minute. He had been patient, more patient than he would ever have dreamt he could be over this woman, and more honest in his opening up to her too. Was she aware of that? Aware he'd let her see more of him than anyone else had done?

Admittedly he hadn't intended that to begin with. His

firm mouth twisted. The evening chats he'd manoeuvred as a means of finding out more about her with a view to getting her into bed had backfired a little. She'd got under his skin, beguiled him, tempted him to reveal things he'd never thought he'd talk about to anyone. Not because she'd been pushy, hell no, just the opposite. It was the gentle, unassuming way she had that had knocked him for six. That and the air of unsophisticated innocence that clothed her like a second skin. He'd had to remind himself more than once that she had been married, that she had two children and was far from being a chaste virgin.

But when he kissed her… His body stirred, becoming as hard as a rock. She was a different woman. And he wanted her—sinner and saint, he wanted all of her.

It was the damnedest thing, he reflected as he drove home through the white, frosty world outside the cosy warmth of the car, that he—a man who placed great value on being in control—had never felt more out of control in his life. And yet it didn't make any difference. She was like a drug and infinitely more addictive than the strongest narcotic or opiate.

When he drew up outside her house it was past eleven o'clock and only the hall light was glowing. He kissed her awake, smiling slightly as he felt her respond even before she was fully conscious.

She was flushed and dishevelled and as sexy as every schoolboy fantasy by the time he exited the car and walked round to the passenger door, and once she was standing on the pavement he kissed her again, lightly, before looking down at her face in the shadows. He brought his hand up and traced her lips with a finger. 'Are you going to tell your parents about us?'

She blinked. 'That we're friends?'

He grinned. 'Your mother likes me,' he said with an air of considerable satisfaction.

'Only because you ate two helpings of her casserole.'

'When am I going to be invited again?'

She'd fallen into that one, Toni thought wryly. 'I don't know. How often do friends eat at each other's homes?'

'*All* the time.'

'Steel—'

He caught the note of anxiety in her voice with his lips as he kissed her. 'A day at a time, sweetheart. OK?'

She swallowed. Now she was home, standing outside the place wherein her two children lay sleeping, she was filled with doubts and panic. This could only end badly. She knew it as surely as night followed day. So why on earth was she allowing it to continue for another moment? And then she looked up into the hard, handsome face and she knew why. *At some point over the last six months she had fallen in love with Steel.*

She lowered her lids to hide the stricken look she knew must be visible in her eyes. She had fought against it, railed against it, told herself all sorts of lies and evasions, but it was still true. She loved him. She loved him as she would never love anyone else, the infatuation she had felt for Richard before they had married a pale shadow in comparison.

A tiny part of her acknowledged it was a relief to admit it to herself at last; a far bigger part felt terrified.

'You're tired. I'd better let you go.' This time his kiss was just a peck on the top of her nose. 'And tell your mother you've invited me to dinner tomorrow.'

'I haven't. I didn't,' she said weakly, without heat.

'Or I'll phone up and tell her myself. I'm in your life, Toni. Get used to it.'

She watched him turn and walk back to his car and she thought, Yes, but for how long? How long before the novelty of him having to chase a woman for once— because that was undoubtedly what this was all about— began to pall? However long it was, it wouldn't be long enough. She wanted for ever. The whole roses-round-the-door scenario. Stupid, stupid, stupid.

She became aware that although he was sitting in the car he was waiting to see her inside the house before he drove off. It was one of the many little courtesies that were as natural to him as breathing and her heart ached with love for him. She waved once and then opened the front door and stepped into the house, closing it and leaning against it as she heard the engine purr into life.

She continued to stand there long after the sound of the car had disappeared, a thousand and one emotions tearing at her breast. And then very slowly, like an old woman, she climbed the stairs to check on the girls. They were fast asleep, Amelia lying with one hand under her cheek and Daisy curled into a little ball under the covers with only the top of her head visible. Her precious babies, her precious girls.

And only then did she let the tears come.

She was awoken from a deep sleep by her mobile phone, which she'd forgotten to turn off the night before. Half falling off the small sofa bed she staggered across the sitting room and reached for her bag, aware it was still dark. 'Hello?' she said muzzily. 'Who is it?'

'Toni? I'm an uncle.' Steel's voice was ridiculously excited. 'Annie had a little girl this morning.'

'Oh, Steel.' Suddenly she was wide awake. 'How wonderful.'

'She's beautiful, exquisite, with the tiniest fingers and toes. I can't believe she was inside her mother only yesterday.'

'You've seen her already?' Toni squinted at the time on her mobile and it informed her it was five o'clock.

'I've been at the hospital since I left you. Just as I drove away Jeff phoned and said Annie had been in labour all day and they were leaving for the hospital, and if I could spare half an hour she'd love to see me. So I went and saw her and then waited in a little room until the baby was born. She's perfect. Small but perfect.'

'What did she weigh?' Toni asked, smiling at his enthusiasm.

'Six pound something, I think.'

'Is she still Eve?'

'Almost. It's Miranda Eve now. Miranda was our mother's name,' he added huskily. 'It suits her already.'

For a moment the urge to see him and hold him in her arms was so strong she felt weak with it. He was upset; thrilled but upset, and she could understand that. His mother would never see her granddaughter. That was hard at such a joyous time.

'Where are you now?' she said softly.

'Sitting outside your house.'

'*What?*' She jumped as though he'd walked into the sitting room, smoothing down her hair hastily.

'I—I wanted to be near you,' he said hoarsely.

Oh, Steel, Steel. You are going to break my heart. 'Fancy a coffee?' she whispered. 'But you'll have to be quiet. The girls have got elephant ears.'

'A mouse wouldn't make less noise,' he whispered back.

'I'll let you in.' She could tell he was smiling.

Hastily switching the light on, she delved into her handbag for her brush and brought some sort of order to her hair. Her face was shiny with sleep and devoid of make-up but she couldn't do anything about that, she reflected as she stared into the sitting-room mirror. Reaching for her thick towelling robe, she pulled it on over her thin silk pyjamas, knotting the belt tightly. She had cried herself to sleep last night, wondering how she was going to cope with seeing him at the office with other people around for the first time since his amazing declaration, but now at least there was only the two of them and Annie's baby would break the ice. Not that there was ice between them. Just the opposite. It was fire every time their lips touched. Which was the cause of all her problems.

'Hi. Thanks for letting me come in.'

She had opened the door to find him on the doorstep, incredibly sexy if a little tired, black stubble coating his chin and his hair falling across his forehead. He looked... She gave up trying to find a word that encapsulated heaven on earth and prayed for self-control. 'Hi yourself.' She swung the door wide as she turned and walked through the hall to the kitchen. 'I'll put the coffee on.'

'I woke you,' he murmured as he stood in the kitchen doorway.

'Considering it's five o'clock in the morning, is that surprising?' She turned and smiled to soften the words. 'Sit down, you look exhausted.' *And what power decreed that when men looked all in they were ten times more sexy, whereas women just looked haggard?* Few things in life were fair.

He didn't sit down. Instead he walked across and

drew her gently into his arms. They stood quietly, in benign contrast to all their earlier blazing embraces, as he said, 'She's so tiny and so vulnerable, a little scrap of nothing and yet a person with eyelashes and finger-nails. And she looks like Annie. I can remember when Annie was born and I went to see her with my father. I was twelve years old at the time and thought she was the most beautiful thing I'd ever seen. And Miranda is like her. I'd forgotten about that time until today.'

'And Annie's OK?' she asked unsteadily, touched at his emotion.

'She's euphoric. On cloud nine and refusing to come down.'

Toni nodded. 'I can remember when the twins were born, I was the same. And yet scared too. Suddenly I had these two little people who were wholly dependent on me and I was terrified I'd let them down.'

'And you coped with them on your own,' he said, very softly.

Toni had wrapped her arms round his waist and now it took a great deal not to pull away and defuse what was a deeply personal memory. A host of memories. 'Yes, I did, from day one,' she said after a moment or two. 'Richard didn't even come into the hospital with me when I gave birth; he said hospitals made him feel sick. It was a full twenty-four hours before he saw the girls and I found myself making excuses for him to the other women in the maternity unit, pretending he'd been called away at work. The first time he saw them in their little plastic cots by the side of my bed, I could tell he didn't know what to say. For months, years, I tried to tell myself he'd been overcome with the miracle of it, at these two little people who were now suddenly in the world, but in actual fact he felt nothing. In fact the whole business repelled him.'

'Did he say that?' Steel's arms had tightened round her as she'd been talking.

'Yes, one night when we were having a fight about how little he was at home. He—he called them parasites.'

'Hell.' Steel jerked against her.

'It was a couple of months before he died, and from that night I knew our marriage was over. But there were the girls and he was their father... I didn't know what to do.'

'It's OK.' His arms tightened still more and she felt his lips against her forehead.

'They are my beautiful, precious girls, Steel, and he spoke about them as though...' She dragged in a breath. 'I could have killed him that night. If I'd had a weapon in my hands I would have used it.'

He moved her slightly, cupping her face in his hand, his thumb stroking the pure line of her silky cheek. 'Broken kneecap job at the very least, I'd say.'

She gave a damp smile. 'I'm sorry, you don't want to hear this now, not when you're so pleased about Annie.'

He ignored this. 'How come you're not still hating the guy?' he asked quietly. 'Because you don't hate him, do you?'

'I did for a while, even after he'd died. And then one day I realised he was the one who had missed out. The girls had done or said something, I can't even remember what now, and it dawned on me I meant the world to them. For every little bit of love I gave them I got it back tenfold, and Richard had never, would never, experience that. They didn't miss him—in fact they barely noticed he'd gone. And that was terribly sad. He was a stranger to them, a distant cold stranger who had as little impact on their lives as the man in the moon. It—it made me all the more determined to make sure no one would ever let them down again. They deserve the best.'

'Hence the repelling of all boarders on the good ship, Toni George?' The words could have been taken as light; the way he was looking at her was anything but.

'I guess.' She smiled wanly. 'Yes.'

He stroked the tears from her face with large male hands. 'You're some woman.' He pulled her into him again, his voice a rumble above her head as he said, 'We came across each other too soon, didn't we? You'd barely had time to come to terms with the fact you were free and then I was there.'

His insight surprised her. But it was true. And then she wondered if his words were a form of farewell. She couldn't blame him if he was backing off so soon; he could have any woman he wanted. Why would he put his hand up for getting involved with someone who was little more than a nutcase?

'You mentioned coffee?' He placed his palms along either side of her face. 'And if there's any toast to go with that I wouldn't say no. I'm absolutely starving.'

She had just prepared a pot of coffee and a plate of buttered toast when little footsteps alerted her to the fact the twins were up and about. Sure enough a few moments later two small figures clad in teddy-bear pyjamas appeared in the kitchen doorway and huge brown eyes stared questioningly.

'Well, hello.' Steel smiled at the two little girls who had hesitated on the threshold, clearly unsure of their welcome once they saw him. 'I've just called to show your mummy a picture of my niece who was born this

morning. Would you like to see it too?' he added as he
fetched a camera from his coat pocket. 'She's only an
hour or two old—how about that?'

They sidled over to him, Amelia leading the way as
normal, and stared wide-eyed at the pictures he showed
them.

'She's very tiny.' Amelia studied the camera with intense concentration. 'And her face is all screwed up.'

'And she hasn't got any hair,' Daisy put in. 'Not even
a bit.'

'Not yet, but that will come.' Steel smiled at the girls.
'One day she'll be as pretty as you.'

The twins looked doubtful. 'Has she got a mummy
and a daddy?' Amelia asked after a moment or two.

Steel nodded. 'A very nice mummy and daddy.'

'We've just got a mummy,' Daisy informed him. 'Our
daddy's in heaven and he's not coming back.'

Toni had just browned some more toast and now she
froze, not knowing what to say to help Steel.

'I think your mummy's terrific,' Steel said quietly,
'better than any other mummy I know, which makes you
very lucky, and I think she's probably got some toast for
you right now.'

'Yes! Yes!' Hot buttered toast was the twins' favourite.

It was Daisy who said—once the girls had a slice of
toast each—'Can we sit with you?' as she stood in front
of Steel, all brown-eyed entreaty.

'I don't see why not.' Steel made room for the girls on
each knee, careless of his designer suit and the dripping
butter.

Toni looked into the chiselled male face and knew
she would love him for ever. Which was terrifying.

By the time Toni's parents made an appearance the

twins had already been upstairs to inform their grand-parents the steel man was in the kitchen having break-fast. Consequently Vivienne and William were remark-ably matter-of-fact, congratulating Steel on becoming an uncle when he showed them the pictures of Miranda and acting as though it were commonplace to have a multimillionaire eating breakfast in their tiny kitchen.

Every moment was bittersweet for Toni. It was impos-sible not to imagine how it would be if the twins were Steel's children, his flesh and blood, because he was so good with them and they seemed to have taken to him big time. For such a masculine man he definitely had a way with children, and she found this surpris-ing, although she reflected she shouldn't have. He had brought Annie up, hadn't he? And she'd noticed he had a compassion for anything small and defenceless, even going to the bother of catching a spider and putting it outside when one had found its way into his office a few weeks back. On the other hand he was ruthless and uncompromising in business, annihilating the competi-tion without any remorse and showing no weakness.

An enigma. She nodded mentally to the thought as she and the girls disappeared upstairs to wash and get dressed. Steel had suggested he give her a lift. He just needed to visit his apartment to change his clothes and have a shave first, he'd said blandly, as though the two of them arriving at the office together would provoke no comment.

Once the girls were ready for school they disappeared downstairs again leaving her to finish getting ready. By the time she came down they were jumping with excite-ment owing to the fact Steel had suggested he take them to the school's breakfast club in his car.

'It's called a Rapide,' Amelia informed Toni very

seriously. 'Because it goes fast. An' it goes really, *really* fast, doesn't it?' she added, turning to Steel.

'Like the wind,' he assured the little girl gravely.

'But not when it's taking you two to school,' Toni cautioned. 'Then it goes nice and safely.'

'Oh, *Mummy*.' She was clearly the spoilsport this morning.

Toni could just feel the neighbours' eyes boring into her back when she and Steel and the girls climbed into the car a few minutes later. Curtains were twitching and no doubt speculation would be rife. And this was just the beginning of it. Steel was larger than life in every respect and consequently people took a healthy—and not so healthy—interest in what he did. Mind, she supposed she bought the celebrity gossip mags now and again, which perhaps wasn't so very different.

As luck would have it—bad luck—the first person Toni saw when she got out of the car with the girls was Poppy with Nathan. Poppy's husband usually dropped Nathan off every morning on his way to work to save Poppy having to try and get the other three children dressed and out of the house so early—no mean feat since the new baby had arrived.

'Graham's taken a couple of days' holiday so I can get on with some Christmas shopping without the kids,' Poppy said as Toni reached her, talking to Toni but with her eyes fixed on the Aston Martin. 'Is that him? Steel Landry?'

'Uh-huh.' Toni continued walking to the school gate but once the children had gone in Poppy caught hold of her arm. 'You sly old fox, you. What's going on?'

'Nothing.' She didn't feel ready to discuss Steel this morning.

'Nothing? He's dropping your children off and you

say nothing?' Poppy's eyes sparkled. 'Did he stay the night?'

'He called by early this morning, that's all, and offered me a lift, and Amelia and Daisy wanted a ride in his car. That's all there is to it. And—and we're probably going to have the odd date now and again, just as friends.'

Poppy stopped dead and then as Toni carried on walking hurried to catch her up. 'Since when has all this happened? You didn't say a word about it at the weekend.'

'Since yesterday. We—we had a heart-to-heart.'

They had almost reached the car and as Steel leant across from the driver's seat and thrust open the passenger door for Toni to climb in Poppy shamelessly stared. Toni couldn't help smiling. She thought it was the first time she'd seen Poppy lost for words. But only for a moment. *'Eye candy,'* Poppy murmured, 'doesn't do him justice.'

'Shh, he'll hear you.'

'Ring me,' said Poppy as Toni slid into the car. 'Soon.'

# CHAPTER NINE

Toni willed Steel to start the car quickly; she wouldn't put it past Poppy to open the door and ask for Steel's autograph!

Poppy was still blatantly staring as they drew away, and it was a moment before Steel drawled, 'Eye candy?'

'You heard.' She blushed a cherry red. 'I'm so sorry.'

'I didn't know women spoke in those terms.'

'Poppy does.' And I'll strangle her later.

'And you? Do you think I'm eye candy?'

Toni nerved herself to look at him, but could read nothing from the expressionless profile. 'I think you're a good-looking man,' she said primly.

'Thank you very much, fair maiden. My ego remains intact.' He grinned at her before pulling into the deserted car park of a builders' merchant that wasn't yet open. Cutting the engine, he reached across and turned her head towards him by a gentle hand on her chin. 'Do you want to know what I think about you? You're the most beautiful, fascinating, sexy, complete woman I've ever met. And the most puzzling and frustrating. But I'm getting to grips with the puzzle now.'

His voice had been deep and warm and very sensual,

and she shivered, but not from the cold morning. And when he had completed the puzzle, what then? Was that when he grew bored and walked away? She had seen a photograph of his last girlfriend in the paper a few weeks ago, Barbara something or other. She had won a big court case and her gorgeous face had been splashed all across the tabloids. Someone in the office had thrust it under her nose and as she'd stared at the laughing woman in the photograph she'd felt her heart sink, although she hadn't allowed herself to question why. Barbara had been stunning and acutely intelligent to boot, the epitome of the sort of wonder woman who might just manage to hang onto someone like Steel. Only she hadn't. And so what chance would a mere mortal have?

'Toni?' Steel's voice brought her out of her whirling thoughts. 'What is it? What's wrong?'

'Nothing.' She forced a smile. 'I was just thinking none of those adjectives fit me, that's all.'

'If any other woman said that to me I'd think they were angling for more compliments, but you actually mean it, don't you?' He shook his head, his silver-blue eyes stroking over her face. 'I'm going to build up that self-esteem until you'll expect to bowl everyone over when you walk into a room, just like you do me.'

'Oh, Steel.' She couldn't help smiling.

'You're delicious, woman.' His voice was muffled as he leant across and nuzzled her throat, causing her pulse to pound in reaction. 'And you wear the sexiest perfume. I catch a whiff of that in the office and I lose the plot entirely.'

'Steel, you *never* lose the plot.' Her voice was husky. He was dropping little burning kisses over her throat and chin as he worked up to her mouth.

He took her lips and kissed her long and hard before he said, 'It's a regular occurrence since you came to work for me. I see you sitting demurely at your desk working away and all I can think of is how you'd look spread out on it being ravaged. You'll walk into my office for a minute or two and then it takes me an hour to get control again. I want to take you on the sofa in my office, on the floor, hell, anywhere. I'm obsessed with you, woman. Don't you know that?'

She was entranced by his idea of her as a femme fatale, but still felt as though it were another woman he was talking about. Richard's love-making had always been brief and perfunctory, an exercise to relieve himself of a bodily need. She'd often felt a blow-up doll would have served him just as well for all the interest he actually took in her, as a woman. His lack of interest had chipped away at her self-confidence in her femininity more than she'd realised.

'You're gorgeous, Toni, and all woman.' It was as though he could read her mind. 'I can't get enough of you.'

Her soft sigh shuddered through her body as he pulled her into him, kissing her again, and then as he caught himself on part of the car he swore softly. 'If anyone had told me a few months ago I'd be necking in the front seat of my car I'd have laughed at them. One day I'm going to have you exactly where I want you. You know that, don't you?'

He slid fully into his seat as he spoke, starting the engine and pulling out of the car park as the first employee drove in.

They drove straight to Steel's apartment. She hadn't been there since her interview months ago, and it was as beautifully indifferent as she remembered, right down to the bowls of hothouse blooms arranged about the sitting room. She glanced round and then started as Steel put his arms round her middle, nuzzling the back of her neck as he said, 'You were frowning—why?'

She spoke the truth. 'The plans I've got for that lovely old house are nothing like this. You do realise that, don't you? Are you sure you want me to have a free hand?'

'Never been so sure of anything in my life.' He turned her round to face him, his eyes glowing a deep silver made all the more striking by his thick lashes and the black stubble coating the lower part of his face. 'And I told you, the house is to be a home. This place is convenient but it's never really been that.'

It was slowly dawning on her that she had the right to touch him, to act like a girlfriend, and now she placed her palms along either side of his face. This man had swept away all the rules she'd made for herself when Richard had died and she knew she was playing with fire, but she couldn't help herself.

His day-old beard was sandpapery against the soft skin of her fingers, and he smiled as she grimaced. 'I know, I'm rough.'

She touched the odd grey hair in the jet black; he was greying slightly at his temples too and it suited him, adding a devastating maturity to his sexiness. 'Silver threads,' she murmured. 'And very distinguished too.'

'I'm thirty-eight years old, Toni. Thirty-nine in the New Year. Does that worry you?' He was suddenly very serious.

'Worry me?' She didn't understand. 'Why would it worry me?'

'I'm eight years older than you.'

'My father is ten years older than my mother, as it

happens. They used to laugh about it when I was growing up. My mother's always called him her sugar daddy.'

He grinned the grin that had the power to make her weak at the knees as he released her. 'I'll go and freshen up. Make some coffee, would you? You'll find everything somewhere in the kitchen.' He waved a vague hand.

She took off her coat and left it with her handbag on one of the sofas, wandering through to the kitchen as Steel disappeared. The kitchen was amazing, all stainless steel, pale maple wood and glittering black granite worktops, with an Italian porcelain floor Toni knew would have cost an arm and a leg. Here, though, Maggie's touch was evident. A pile of cookery books next to the fabulous stove, an apron slung over the back of a chair and a row of fresh herbs in little glass containers on the window sill. Homely touches to soften the show-room perfection.

She dug and delved and managed to have the coffee poured out and waiting when Steel strolled into the kitchen a few minutes later, shaved and hair still damp from the shower. He was wearing a brilliant white shirt, unbuttoned, and tailored black trousers, and he was barefoot.

Toni took one look and knew she was lost. The next stage of their relationship was going to progress as fast as wildfire and right now, she thought as she walked straight into his open arms. He didn't kiss her at once, simply holding her against him as he looked deeply into her eyes. 'I've missed you while I've been gone,' he murmured lazily, his eyes smiling into hers.

She giggled, wrapping her arms round his lean waist. 'You've only been gone five minutes.'

'Five minutes is five lifetimes if I can't see you,

touch you, taste you. What have you done to me? I'm a wreck.'

'Not you, Steel Landry.'

'Yes, me. You've got me tied up in knots.' His voice was rueful and she realised with a bolt of breathtaking amazement he was speaking the truth. For the first time she took the initiative, standing on tiptoe and covering his lips with hers.

His response was immediate. He kissed her with such hunger, such explosive warmth that Toni was instantly swept away on a tide of desire. She gave herself up to the sheer delight of sliding her hands over the rippling muscles beneath the silk of his shirt, tangling her fingers in the covering of black body hair on his chest and luxuriating in the breadth and power in the big male body holding her. Steel pulled her closer, so close their bodies were practically fusing together, curves melting into hard, angular planes. It was intoxicating, thrilling and what she had been born for.

Toni inhaled the clean smell of lemon on his skin from the soap he'd used during his shower; it mingled with the musky scent that was all his to produce an intoxicating aphrodisiac she was powerless to resist, and when he moved her against him so she could feel every inch of his arousal she moaned softly in her throat.

Her body heat released her own perfume. The magnolia and summer fruits, coupled with her own personal fragrance, aroused Steel still more if that was possible, and he was almost devouring her. The soft wool dress she was wearing clung to her body like a second skin as he ran his hands over her breasts, her tiny waist, the firm smooth line of her hips.

Toni's eyes were closed and she felt a tight congestion in her belly as the pleasure mounted, and even though she knew where this was leading, where it would end, she made no effort to stop him. She didn't want to. She wanted him to undress her, to make love to her. She wanted to feel him inside her, possessing her. She wanted…everything.

It came as a drenching shock when he tore his mouth from hers a moment later, steadying her swaying body with his hands on her arms before taking a step backwards. She opened dazed eyes, her pupils dilated with the raw passion that still showed in her face, unable to believe that he had stopped.

Steel was breathing hard, his breath ragged as he muttered, 'Maggie,' tucking his shirt into his trousers as he spoke.

'What?' She stared at him uncomprehendingly, and then she heard the sound of a tune being hummed seconds before Steel's daily appeared in the kitchen doorway.

Steel had had the presence of mind to start pouring coffee and now he turned, his voice remarkably controlled as he said, 'Morning, Maggie.'

Maggie appeared as flustered as Toni felt, stopping a step into the room and looking from one to the other. 'I'm sorry,' she said quickly. 'I didn't expect— I mean, you're never here at this time of the morning.'

'I've been at the hospital all night.' Steel handed a cup of coffee to both women as he spoke, completely his normal, urbane self. 'Annie had a daughter in the early hours and I called in Toni's to tell her and then offered her a lift into work once I'd washed and shaved.'

'A daughter? There, didn't I tell you it would be a little girl? I'm never wrong about these things.' Maggie smiled at Toni. 'Never got one wrong in my life.'

'Who needs scans when they've got you, Maggie?'

Steel took a long pull at his own coffee and Toni was gratified to see he wasn't as in control as he'd like them to believe. His hand was shaking just the slightest.

For herself she couldn't believe how close she had come to making love with him right there on the kitchen floor. The way it had been she doubted if they would have made it to the bedroom. And Maggie knew. In spite of how tactful the little woman was being, bustling over to the stove as she asked Steel if they'd like a cooked breakfast, Toni had seen the speculative gleam in Maggie's eyes.

Excusing herself, she made her way into the little cloakroom off the hall and shut the door before looking at herself in the mirror. She groaned softly. Of course Maggie knew. The woman staring back at her out of the mirror looked as though she had been ravished. Her lips were red and swollen, her cheeks were flushed and her eyes bright, and her hair...

After splashing cold water on her face she smoothed her hair into order with her hands, having left her bag, which held her brush, in the sitting room. She stood for a few moments with her eyes shut and her forehead pressed against the cold glass as she pulled herself together. Only twenty-four hours ago she had started the day thinking Steel was driving her to a new project he wanted her to oversee. Well, he had, in a way, but so much had happened since then she felt that Toni had been a different person and bore no resemblance to the woman she was now.

When she walked back to the kitchen Maggie was busy dishing up a full English breakfast. In spite of having had two pieces of toast with Steel and the girls, Toni found she was suddenly ravenously hungry. The three of them ate at the kitchen table, the winter sunlight pouring in the window picking up blue lights in Steel's jet-black hair. Out of nowhere, Toni found herself saying, 'Your colouring is very unusual, the black hair and light eyes. Is Annie's the same?'

'See for yourself later. I thought we'd call in the hospital for a few minutes when we leave here. I'd like to take her some flowers and it will give you a chance to meet her and see the baby.'

Toni saw Maggie's eyes flash over their faces but the small woman made no comment, gathering up the dirty plates and stacking them in the dishwasher, before asking if they'd like more coffee. Steel took his with him into the bedroom where he continued getting ready and Toni sat with Maggie in the kitchen, listening to her chatter about the preparations for Christmas and a hundred and one other things besides. Maggie was one of those folk who could talk for England and rarely required a comment on what she was saying, and it was surprisingly restful in the circumstances.

As they left the apartment building it was bitterly cold after the centrally heated warmth within and Toni shivered. Steel pulled her into him, wrapping his arm round her waist and kissing the top of her head as they walked to the car.

Somehow, after all the passionate embraces they'd exchanged, it was more intimate than anything that had gone before. Intimate and poignant. This closeness was a transitory thing. One day it would be another woman on his arm and she must remember that. Must try to protect herself from giving too much emotionally.

It was a ridiculous thought and she acknowledged its futility in the next breath. She loved him. There was no protection against love. The deeper you went, the more it took over.

The private hospital where Steel was paying for Annie to have her baby was only a minute away by car from the apartment, but it was already past ten o'clock when a starched and somewhat imperious nurse escorted them to Annie's room. Steel had phoned Fiona from the apartment to tell her not to expect the pair of them at the office until after lunch, and Toni wondered what the other woman had thought. She might assume they were on site at one of the various projects going on, but on the other hand... But she couldn't worry about what people thought; there was no point. Gossip and speculation were par for the course for any woman associated with Steel.

When they walked into the bright, cheerful little room that was so unlike National Health hospitals' colour schemes of green or brown or grey, Toni saw a dark-haired girl sitting up in bed reading a magazine with an open box of chocolates on her knees.

'Steel!' Annie's face lit up. 'And don't tell me, this must be Toni. I feel I know you already, Steel's told me so much about you.'

'Has he?' Toni couldn't hide her surprise.

Annie didn't appear to notice, smiling a smile that was a feminine version of Steel's. 'It's so nice to meet you at last. Come and sit down.'

Toni glanced at the see-through plastic crib holding a tiny shape that was squirming and making snuffling noises.

'Do you want to hold her?' Annie offered. 'She's due for a feed soon so she's waking up. Now's a good time.'

'I'd love to.' Toni bent over the crib, inhaling the sweet powdered scent emanating from the little bundle, and carefully picked the baby up. 'She's so tiny and so beautiful,' she whispered, sitting down on the chair Steel pushed forwards and cradling Miranda Eve in her arms. 'It seems another age since my girls were this size.'

'They're twins, aren't they? What did they weigh when they were born?' Annie asked, her eyes—a deeper blue than Steel's—soft as they stroked over her child.

'Amelia was exactly six pounds and Daisy was nearly five; I resembled an elephant in the month before the birth, but they were healthy and strong so nothing else mattered.'

Steel was standing, leaning against the wall as he watched her with the baby, his eyes silver slits in the sunlight slanting into the room. He had placed the enormous basket of white and pink rosebuds they had picked up from the florist shop across the road to the hospital on the long broad shelf that ran the length of one wall, between two bouquets standing in vases of water. 'I take it those are from Jeff,' he said, indicating the huge arrangement of deep red roses, which had a somewhat garish plastic gold heart attached to the cellophane. 'Who are the carnations and lilies from?' The second bouquet was more extravagant than the first and a vision of colour.

Annie hesitated. 'Barbara,' she said reluctantly.

Steel straightened, but his voice was expressionless when he said, 'Barbara? How does Barbara know about the baby?'

Annie shrugged. 'She's rung once or twice during the pregnancy asking how I am; don't ask me why.'

Toni kept her eyes on the baby in her arms. She knew why. The beautiful attorney wanted Steel back and if she could maintain some sort of contact with Annie, it might be a way in.

'Apparently she woke Jeff up this morning at eight

o'clock when he'd only got home from the hospital at six, asking if the baby had arrived. He wasn't best pleased. And the flowers came just before you walked in.'

Steel nodded as Toni glanced up at him. His firm mouth was set uncompromisingly and a muscle was working in his jaw. He was angry. Nevertheless his voice was even and without heat as he changed the subject and asked Annie about the food, even teasing her about the box of chocolates and warning her she wasn't eating for two any more.

They left a short time afterwards so Annie could feed the baby in peace, but before they did so Steel held his niece for a couple of minutes. Toni didn't think anything had hurt her so much in her life. He was so natural with the tiny infant, so blatantly adoring that it was like a knife through Toni's heart. One day he would meet someone who could cope with being with a man like Steel and wouldn't mind the women who flocked round him, would even turn a blind eye to the odd affair as long as it was discreet and he came home to her in the end. Because he would have children. Looking at him holding Miranda, she could see the tiny baby had awakened something in him, something primal and strong.

Once they were sitting in the car in the small hospital car park, Steel didn't start the engine immediately. Turning to look at her, he said quietly, 'What's wrong?'

'Wrong?' She smiled a brittle smile. 'Nothing. The baby's beautiful and Annie's so nice.'

Steel being Steel, he cut through the prevarication. 'Is it because Barbara sent Annie those flowers? I had no knowledge of her contact with my sister, I can promise you that, and I've had nothing to do with her for a long time.'

Toni nodded. 'I believe you,' she said flatly, looking through the windscreen rather than at him.

She was aware of his eyes searching her face. 'Then what's wrong, Toni? Because you're a different woman from the one who walked in that place with me half an hour ago.'

'I told you, nothing's wrong. Everything's fine.'

'OK.' He settled back in his seat. 'I can sit here all day if necessary, all night too, but we're not leaving until you tell me.' He locked the doors as he spoke. 'I mean it.'

'Don't be silly.' She stared at him in alarm. 'Start the car.'

He didn't answer her, switching on the music and making himself comfortable as he shut his eyes.

'Steel, you can't hold me captive here.'

'Funny, but I thought that was exactly what I'm doing.'

Helplessly, she said, 'I don't suppose I liked your ex sending Annie the flowers, OK? That's it. No big deal.'

He sat up, switching off the music, and the silver eyes raked her face. 'No, it's more than that. You're not peeved or irritated, this is something more serious than that, and I can't understand if you won't discuss it.'

'There's nothing *to* understand.'

'Like I said, I can wait all day,' he said lazily, his easy tone catching her on the raw.

Flooded by emotions as chaotic as a winter's storm, Toni met his eyes. 'This is a mistake—us seeing each other, I mean. If it's too difficult to go back to how we were, I'll leave immediately, or I'll finish the new project first, if that's what you would prefer.'

'What the hell are you talking about?' He wasn't shouting, but the lazy note had gone, to be replaced by a softness that was dangerous. 'You're not going anywhere.'

'Yes, Steel. I am.' Her chin came up and her mouth thinned. 'And you can't tell me what I can or can't do. No one can do that any more. That ended with Richard's death.'

'This is to do with him, isn't it? The louse you married? You're frightened of being with someone again, of feeling something for a man.' He shook his head. 'I'm no Richard, Toni.'

*Feeling* something? He couldn't have said anything more guaranteed to make her mad. She loved him, she had been struggling with her feelings for months and driving herself half mad in the process, and he talked about her being frightened of *feeling* something? Her fingers tightened, whitening her knuckles. 'This is absolutely nothing to do with Richard and all to do with you,' she said with such transparent honesty he couldn't fail to believe her. 'I don't want to be absorbed into your lifestyle, Steel. To have to try and become the sort of woman you need.'

'I haven't the faintest idea what you're talking about, dammit,' he bit out through clenched teeth. He had to stop for a long calming breath. 'You don't have to try and be anything, just yourself. Is this about Barbara, Toni? The woman means nothing to me—surely you know that?'

It was an unfortunate choice of words but he couldn't have known that. Toni stared at him. Her voice was quiet now and infinitely sad. 'You were with this woman, you shared each other's lives, you slept with her, and not so very long ago either. Just a matter of months. And now you say she means nothing to you? That's exactly what I mean, Steel. One day it will be me you're saying that about.'

His head jerked at the accusation. His eyes blazing silver sparks, he ground out, 'Never.'

'And there are so many Barbaras out there, Steel. Beautiful women, available women, women who will throw themselves at you and not take no for an answer. You're…irresistible.'

'And you're saying I have as little emotional maturity as a stud stallion, is that it? All these women who will supposedly throw themselves into my arms I'll service without thinking twice about it? I'm a man, Toni. Not an animal. I don't take a lady because she indicates she's available. Before I met you I had my share of women, but I've never denied that or made a secret of it. But it wasn't a conveyor belt, dammit. And neither was it all about sex. Surprising as it obviously is to you, I do require mental as well as physical stimulation when I'm with a woman.'

'That doesn't surprise me. It's just that there are so many women who will want you who are more beautiful and more intelligent than me. I wasn't enough for—for Richard, and he was an ordinary man. You're not an ordinary man, Steel.'

He searched her face, seeking an explanation that wasn't there, a way to get through to her. 'You cut me and I bleed,' he said softly. 'The same as the next man. And your ex was an addict always in search of his next fix. The addiction had nothing to do with you as a person, a woman. Aphrodite herself wouldn't have been able to change the way he thought and acted. It was a sickness, Toni. A sickness that controlled and manipulated him until he danced to its tune. That's the way all addiction works.'

She sat, straight-backed and deathly pale. 'Like I said before, this is nothing to do with Richard.'

'The hell it isn't.' A vein in his neck throbbed beneath the surface of his skin. 'He's made you afraid, afraid to trust your instincts, your emotions, what you feel. He's crippled you, but in a worse way than if he'd knocked you about.'

'Don't talk about me as though I'm a victim.'

'Then don't act like one!'

His explosive exclamation caused her stomach muscles to contract but no sign of it showed on her face. She remained perfectly still, a flesh and blood statue.

'When we first met you told me you didn't want a man around because of the twins. You didn't want them "let down" again, remember? But that was an excuse, whether you admit it or not. Deep down it was yourself you were protecting, not them.'

'How dare you!' She reared up like an enraged tigress, all pretence of calm gone. 'You know nothing about it.'

'Oh, I dare, Toni. This is our future, yours and mine, I'm fighting for. The gloves are off. You've just called me a womaniser and a no-hoper, the sort of guy who will take everything on offer and enjoy the ride.'

'I did not,' she protested furiously. 'I never said any such thing.'

'Virtually.' His eyes had turned an icy mother-of-pearl.

'No. I said women will always throw themselves at you and there's not a man alive who won't respond to that eventually.'

'Wrong. You're looking at him.'

She went on as if he hadn't spoken. 'I don't want that sort of pressure when I'm with someone, that's what I'm saying. Maybe ninety-nine per cent of women could cope with it, but I'm me and—and I don't want to.'

'One bouquet and I'm hung, drawn and quartered?'

Under the anger there was a bewilderment that wrenched at her heart but she couldn't weaken now. This relationship had already gone too far. He had permeated her life like the steady drip-drip of water in a cavern, innocuous in itself but with the power to form mighty stalactites and stalagmites. The more she had got to know him, the more she had liked what she'd discovered, which made him a very dangerous man, and if she slept with him, if she opened up her body as well as her heart, she would be lost. She would never be able to walk away from him. And say what he might, she *was* thinking of the twins too. They'd had one male role model in their young lives who, if he had lived, could have given them a distorted view of family life and love that might have affected them for ever. Fate had saved them from that and she had a duty not to put them in harm's way again.

'You're wrong about me,' Steel said quietly after a full minute had ticked by in screaming silence. 'I'm like the guy in one of the Sunday school stories we were told as kids, the one who sold everything he had to buy the pearl of great price.'

Toni couldn't argue any more. He'd never understand and they had no meeting point. She lowered her head, hating the fact her hands were trembling and hoping Steel hadn't noticed. 'I'm sorry,' she whispered, all anger and indignation gone. 'I'm not as strong as I thought I was. You're right, it only took one bouquet. But there would be other bouquets, other women through the months and years looking for a way to get your attention. I don't have a thick skin, Steel, and I wouldn't be able to laugh such incidents off, regardless of how you might react. I—I'm not made that way.'

She expected him to say more, to fight his corner. Instead, after a long tense moment he started the engine, saying quietly, 'I would like you to complete the new project before you leave. Is that acceptable?'

She forced her numb lips to move. 'Of course.'

'Thank you.'

*It was over.*

# CHAPTER TEN

'I'M SORRY, TONI, BUT I think you're stark staring mad.' Poppy stared at her with something approaching horror. 'He's the most gorgeous man on the planet and absolutely loaded, and by your own admission he was great with the twins and they adored him, and you give him the old heave-ho. And not because you've caught him cheating or anything, but simply because other women find him attractive. Don't you think that's a teensy bit unreasonable?'

Toni shook her head. She'd been hoping Poppy would be sympathetic, but she might have known she'd get the truth, the whole truth and nothing but the truth from her friend. 'It's not as simple as that.'

'Excuse me, but I think it is.' Poppy was standing hands on hips. 'And you like him, don't you? I mean, *really* like him?'

Toni nodded. Understatement of the year.

'Oh, *Toni*. What have you done?' Poppy said sadly.

'Don't.' Toni's voice wobbled. 'I've cried enough already and I don't want the twins to see me upset.'

'They're fine, hark at them.' Amelia and Daisy and Poppy's two boys were playing in the boys' bedroom and, if the shrieks and laughter were anything to go by, were having the time of their lives. Rose was playing at their feet and the baby was asleep.

It was Saturday morning, and the last three days had been the worst of her life. Since their talk in the car park Steel had retreated somewhere very distant. He was still present physically, still polite and courteous when he spoke to her, but it was clear to her she'd achieved her aim and whatever had been between them was dead as far as he was concerned. And following on from this thought, Toni said now in her defence, 'He never spoke of love, you know. Commitment. For ever. It was a sexual thing on his side. Something that would be short-lived and semi-permanent.'

'Even if that was true, and I don't think it was but I'll come on to that in a minute, I'd still say you were the luckiest woman alive. Again by your own admission he was sweet and thoughtful and not at all the big I am, like some men would be in his position, and you'd have had a fabulous time together. He'd have wined and dined you and the bedding part would have been out of this world.'

'Poppy—' She didn't think she could take any more of this.

'But I think it was more than that with him. See it from his side for a moment, Toni. Right from the word go you made it clear you were off limits because of what had happened with Richard and you being a single mother and everything, and so why would the poor guy say anything about for ever with you liable to run screaming if he did? He did the softly-softly routine for your sake. He didn't give into his macho desires and take you on the office desk or in his chair or anywhere else he'd no doubt fantasised about, he let you get to know him, really know him. Now we all know men mostly think with a part of their anatomy a lot lower than their heads, so if he did all that for you I'd say it was more than good old lust driving him. And let's face it, he could have any woman he wanted just by crooking his little finger if it was only sex motivating him.'

'You're not making me feel better. I wanted you to say I'd done the right thing and good riddance.'

'To Steel Landry? No can do. Tell him you've changed your mind,' Poppy urged. 'Cry a bit and fall on his manly chest—they can never resist that, especially if you're saying he was right and you were wrong.'

Toni had thought she'd never smile again, but now the corners of her mouth turned up. 'You look like the backbone of the WI, all home-made jam and sponge cakes and church fetes. How come you're such an out and out vamp under the skin?'

'I could tell you stories about one or two WI members that would make your hair curl,' Poppy said, grinning. 'But seriously, don't let this one slip out of the net. He might have had more than a brief affair on his mind and you'll only know if you give him a chance and chill out a bit.'

Toni gazed at her friend over her coffee cup, her smile dying. 'I love him, Poppy. That's the thing. And whether he wanted me just for a while or something more permanent, I still can't be with him. You've seen him. He's...'

'Oh, yes,' Poppy agreed.

'And rich and powerful—the whole package. I wouldn't know how to go about keeping a man like that. I wouldn't be able to. And then it would be a question of trying to ignore his little...indiscretions, and I'd die, inch by inch.'

'I think you might be doing him an injustice. Who

says he's going to play around? He's drop-dead gorgeous, yes, but even sublime beings like him are allowed to find "the one".'

'And what if I'm not the one? What then?'

Poppy stared at her, suddenly deadly serious. 'I know you love him, but do you trust him?' she said very quietly as the noise upstairs reached new heights. 'You've seen him almost every day for six months and you've worked closely with him on and off. And all those late-night cosies when everyone else had gone home. With all you've learnt about him, do you trust him?'

Toni's eyes were stricken. 'I don't know.'

'Richard undermined you when he was alive and even more when he died and you found out the truth. The male sex suddenly became unreliable and treacherous and devious, I can understand that. Perhaps I shouldn't have asked if you trusted Steel. Perhaps I should have asked if you trust yourself.'

There was suddenly a huge thud upstairs that rocked the ceiling, followed by howls loud enough to wake the baby in her crib by the side of the kitchen table. As Poppy ran upstairs to see what was what Toni picked up the infant and reassured little Rose, who was looking worried. When Poppy came back all four children were in tow, Nathan with an egg-sized lump on his forehead and sniffling, looking very sorry for himself.

'They were playing Superman,' Poppy said ruefully, 'and Nathan tried to "fly" off the top bunk. We're all going to have a drink and a biscuit now, aren't we?' she added to the four subdued children. 'And then we're going to do some nice drawing and colouring at the kitchen table where Mummy and Aunty Toni can keep an eye on you.'

It was the end of further meaningful conversation.

That night as she lay in bed Toni thought about Poppy's last words; they had been very profound, especially considering it had been Poppy speaking. At three in the morning she still hadn't gone to sleep, and at five she gave up all hope of dropping off and got up and made herself a hot drink.

It was bitterly cold outside, the frosted windowpane in the kitchen telling its own story. Snow was forecast in the next few days and everyone was predicting a white Christmas. The kitchen was freezing, the central heating hadn't come on yet, but the chill inside Toni was worse.

She stood at the back door, her hands wrapped round the hot coffee cup as she surveyed Jack Frost's handiwork. Poppy was right. She didn't trust herself any more: her judgement, her self-worth, her discernment—not in matters of the heart anyway. Maybe if she had met Steel five years from now, when she'd had time to sort herself out and get back on an even keel again, it would have been different. But she hadn't. And it wasn't different. She was too frightened of making another huge mistake, and this time she knew she would never recover if it went wrong. So it was better to walk away now. It might be the wrong decision, she'd never know, but, even if it was, it was preferable to staying with him and everything coming unstuck at some time in the future if her worst fears came true. Cowardly it might be, but that was what self-survival came down to sometimes.

By the time the girls came downstairs she was washed and dressed and breakfast was on the table. She was in control again, she told herself firmly. Everything would pan out. Soon she would stop crying when she was in bed at night and feel like eating again. The new project on Steel's house was already underway and she would be spending plenty of time on site; so she wouldn't see much of him, she could make sure of that. He, himself, had made that possible when he'd insisted on giving her carte blanche regarding everything from the alterations and colour schemes to the furniture and fittings.

And once the house was finished—a hard knot formed in her stomach—she would leave; and she had already given Steel a letter of resignation stating this, to which he had agreed with a curt nod of his head as he had read it. She had made some inroad into paying off Richard's debts; the rest would have to happen more slowly when she found another job. All this wasn't the end of the world.

It just felt like it.

Toni worked hard over the next few weeks. She fell into bed each night too exhausted to think, but once she was in dream land her subconscious played all sorts of tricks on her and she couldn't keep Steel at bay. Each morning she awoke feeling more tired than when she had gone to bed, but she forced herself to get up, shower and start the day.

Christmas came and went and the girls were ecstatic when they had a sprinkling of snow on Christmas Eve. Steel gave each employee a Christmas bonus, and when she opened her envelope she could scarcely believe her eyes when she saw the noughts after the ten. 'Ten thousand pounds?' She went straight in to see him, holding the envelope in her hand. 'I didn't expect anything like this. It's too much.'

'Everyone gets a healthy bonus twice a year. It's a good incentive,' he answered, without looking up from the papers he was working on. 'The money is already in your account.'

She stood staring down on the dark head, knowing if she tried to say anything more she'd burst into tears, and then left the room.

He sent Amelia and Daisy parcels through the post too, with a small card saying the exquisite little gold charm bracelets were from the 'steel man'. Toni's mother oohed and ahhed over them to the girls but made no comment to Toni. They'd had to agree to disagree over her finishing with Steel and it was now a forbidden subject. Toni made Christmas special for the girls but she was glad when the 'jolly' season was over, and everyone she came into contact with was miserable because they'd spent too much, eaten too much and drunk too much. It fitted her mood.

The one thing that kept her going, apart from Amelia and Daisy, was the work on Steel's house. She'd fallen in love with the magnificent old cottage and was determined each alteration and each room would be perfect, as the house deserved. This was to be her swansong with Steel's firm and everything had to be right. She wouldn't allow herself to picture Steel living here with another woman, starting a family, enjoying winter evenings together in front of a roaring fire or summer afternoons with cucumber sandwiches and lemonade on the patio while watching the children play in the fresh air. She'd had one day when she had made the mistake of indulging such notions and had got herself into such a state she had been physically sick.

January was a month of heavy blue-grey skies and squalls of blustery sleet and icy rain, but the wave of thick snow that had been forecast way back in December had never materialised. The army of workmen employed on site had meant the project flowed without interruption, and in the first week of February Toni could finally say the job was all but finished.

She'd had intermittent contact with Steel during the last two months. When she was in the office he made no effort seek her out, but when she had to consult with him about something he was always businesslike and agreeable. Once or twice she had caught him staring at her, but there was never any readable expression on his face. As far as she knew he wasn't dating, but he could have been. That was something else she didn't allow herself to think about.

He hadn't actually visited the site once since the day he had taken her there. It was unfortunate that the boss of the building firm she'd contracted for the alterations had an Aston Martin too. A number of times her heart had stopped as she'd heard the car draw up, but it had never been Steel unfurling himself from the sleek interior. Just a paunchy little man who laughed too loudly and stank of BO and garlic.

The day she had set aside for Steel to come and view her work was one of extreme cold and bitter winds. She arrived at the house early in the morning, driving there as soon as she had dropped the girls off at breakfast club.

After checking every cushion was in place and every drape arranged just so, she wandered through to the beautiful drawing room and stood gazing out over the grounds. The frozen landscape intensified every colour and shade, highlighting the few brightly toned leaves clinging to a mature beech tree and the green of the ivy climbing a far wall. The sky had clouded over as she'd been titivating this and that, and there was the smell of snow in the air when she opened the front door to Steel mid-morning.

He smiled at her and a vice gripped her heart. It was the first time for some weeks she had allowed herself the luxury of looking straight at him, and the silver-blue eyes cut through to her soul. He looked wonderful but tired. Definitely tired.

'You have a house to show me, I think?' His voice was warm, relaxed, and yet she thought she detected something else underneath. A tenseness perhaps? Or perhaps it was just excitement. This was to be his home, after all. It was much more important than her previous projects.

He wandered through the downstairs rooms, saying very little. The soft green and cream colour scheme for the drawing room met with his approval, and the taupe and pale lemon for the dining room. The kitchen was now a thing of beauty. When deciding to go all out and make the first reception room into the magnificent drawing room it was always meant to be, Toni had chosen warmer, more family colours for the smaller sitting room. The soft cherry red and mix of dusky pinks made the room cosy and welcoming, a place where children could play and watch TV.

Upstairs each bedroom and en-suite had its own colour scheme, but she was especially pleased with the master bedroom, partly because she felt it was a tribute to her professionalism that she'd made this room as perfect as she could and ignored the fact that Steel might be occupying it with the lady of his choice.

The pale coffee and gold mixed with a blend of oatmeals wasn't overtly masculine or feminine, and she'd taken care the full-length walk-in wardrobe was divided into two distinct halves for the occupants who would share the huge, billowy soft bed, which had been specially made and constructed inside the room and which dominated the space. The drapes that framed the full-length French windows were in the same fabric as the duvet, and the windows opened out onto a stone balcony from which there was a wonderful view over the grounds and the countryside beyond.

Altogether it was a dream of a bedroom, uncompromisingly luxurious from the music system and huge TV down to the concealed fridge holding vintage champagne and a selection of the best wines.

She stood aside for him to enter the room and remained in the doorway as he strolled round, opening the doors onto the balcony and standing there for a moment or two before coming back into the room and shutting the French doors. 'You've created a wonderful home,' he said quietly. 'Now all it needs is the family it was made for.'

She wanted to smile but it was beyond her. Stiffly, she said, 'Thank you. I'm pleased it meets with your approval,' as she stepped backwards onto the wide landing.

He followed her downstairs, and once in the hall took her arm. 'Come into the drawing room a moment. I need to talk to you.'

This was when he formalised her departure. Keeping herself very straight, she walked with him into the elegant reception room and, when he indicated for her to be seated, sat on the edge of one of the cream sofas. She wondered what was different as she'd walked into the room and realised it was snowing: big, fat, feathery flakes falling from a laden sky. The Christmas snow that had been expected had arrived at last.

She had lit a fire earlier in the massive old stone fireplace that blended so well with the beamed ceiling of the gracious room, knowing it would set the room off to perfection for his inspection. Now he walked across and stood with his back to it as he looked at her. 'The envelope on the table,' he said, indicating a large manilla package on the glass coffee table close to the sofa. 'It's yours.'

She nodded. 'I'll take it with me and look at it later.' She couldn't do this right now, not with him standing there reminding her of all she'd given up.

'I'd rather you open it now. There are a couple of things I need to go through with you.'

Numbly she reached for the somewhat bulky package and extracted the papers within. She stared at the top page. The words blurred and danced before her eyes and it was a moment or two before they made sense. Only they didn't. She read the letter through twice and then looked at the wad of papers beneath. Raising her gaze to the silver-blue one watching her so intently, she said dazedly, 'I—I don't understand.'

'It's very simple. I'm giving you the house and those are the relevant papers. I have also deposited an amount in your account to clear your debts and to provide a breathing space while you decide what you want to do from here. I was speaking to James only yesterday and he is very keen to have you back. I understand there will be a vacancy in three months' time when his present interior designer leaves to have a baby. She may return after maternity leave but James is sure they can work out something. You have a life stretching before you free of debt.'

She stared at him. 'I can't accept a house from you.'

'Of course you can. It was always meant for you. Of course at one time I imagined the pair of us in that bedroom upstairs, but—' he shrugged '—your decision changes nothing about the house. Whether we're together or no, it is yours.'

'This is madness.' She felt as though she were in a dream. 'I can't possibly have it, or the money either. You must see that?' She was trembling with shock.

'I see nothing of the kind. You and the twins need your own place and this is a perfect home. It's all arranged.'

'Steel—' She felt as though she were losing her grip on reality. 'This is madness, it's crazy.'

He smiled, but it didn't reach the beautiful eyes and showed how deliberate his air of relaxation was. 'Everyone's allowed to be a little crazy once in their lives. This is my time. It's all official and above board, no strings attached, by the way. All that is required is a few signatures.'

'I can't.' She waved a shaking hand. 'I just can't.'

'I'm not trying to buy you, Toni. I don't work like that. I simply need to know that you and the twins are safe and secure and then we can both get on with our lives. I expect nothing from you, you made it very clear how you feel, but it doesn't change how I feel, OK? So indulge me. You know I can afford to do this without it making a dent in my bank balance, but it would mean a great deal to two little girls and their quality of life. If you can't accept it for yourself, accept it for them. I won't come knocking on your door if that's what's bothering you. Not without an invitation anyway.'

He was bewildering her with his gentleness. 'But why would you do this?' she asked helplessly. 'I don't understand.'

'Isn't it obvious?' He held her frantic gaze.

'Not to me. People don't give other people houses.'

If any other woman of his acquaintance had said

that he wouldn't have believed them, but with Toni he knew it was the truth. He'd been to hell and back the last weeks, but he knew he'd only got himself to blame. In the beginning he had set out to seduce her and yet he'd been the one who had been seduced—seduced into love. Ironic. And the fact that she could walk away from him and cut him out of her life should have killed that love stone dead; he wasn't the type of man to turn the other cheek—he never had been. But it didn't make any difference. It should have, but it didn't, not where she was concerned. She mattered more than his feelings.

His Achilles heel. That was what Jeff had called her when he'd got blind drunk at his brother-in-law's at Christmas and slept the night on their sofa. Jeff had come down early in the morning when he'd had a head on him like a banging drum, and over a cup of strong coffee they'd talked about Toni. Apparently he'd said enough in his inebriated state for Jeff to know most of it anyway.

Steel screened his expression. Jeff had told him that Boxing Day morning to tell her how he felt, just once.

'Forget your pride, mate. She might sling it back in your face but can you feel worse than you do now? Annie's worried sick about you, I can tell you that. Tell her and then leave it in the lap of the gods. If nothing else you'll have no regrets. Say those three words you've always maintained you'll never say to any woman—*I love you*. It's easy, believe me. I say it to Annie all the time.'

Steel walked across to her. He'd known for weeks this day was his last chance to convince her they could make it. Not that he wanted to use the offer of the house as blackmail—he would have done if he'd thought it would work, but he knew Toni too well by now. But it was this

knowledge that told him she cared for him. How much
he didn't know. But she cared.

Toni had risen to her feet at his approach, her eyes
wary, but he didn't touch her. He didn't trust himself to.
'I want you to have the house because I love you,' he said
softly. 'I've never said that to another woman because
it's never been true before. I love you. Completely, utterly, for ever. I need you, I want you and I love you. I
don't want any other woman but you and I never will, but
I can't prove that to you except through time so you'll
have to take it on trust.'

She was ashen-faced. He could have been deliver-
ing a death sentence, the way she was looking at him.
'And—and if I can't?'

'I can help you.'

'Help me?' Toni said wildly, her still façade suddenly
shattering. 'How can you help me when you're the one
person who could destroy me?'

He stared at her. As a declaration of love it left a lot
to be desired, but no words ever sounded sweeter. *She
loved him.* All the agony of the last weeks had been
worth it just for this moment. 'But I won't.' He reached
out and pulled her into his arms and was amazed when
she didn't fight him. 'I want nothing more than to spend
the rest of my life with you. I want to marry you, have
a dozen kids, two dozen. I love you, I love you, I love
you,' he said over and over again, wondering why he'd
thought the words so impossible to say. 'And I'm sorry I
didn't tell you before. I should have. I'm a coward, that's
the truth of it. I thought I was showing you but I should
have said.'

'Steel, don't. Please don't.'

'Marry me, Toni. Live with me. Love me. Let me
love you, and the girls. Make us a family.'

'I can't.' She was sobbing but she still hadn't tried to move out of his arms. 'I can't, don't you see?'

'You can. If you love me, we can do this. Do you love me, Toni? Do you? Tell me?'

'I do love you,' she whispered, her voice breaking. 'That's what scares me. I'm so ordinary—'

'Never say that.' He covered her mouth in a hungry kiss, crushing her against his chest. 'You're beautiful, my pearl beyond price.' In seconds they were lost to the world, straining into each other with an urgency made all the more desperate for their estrangement of the last weeks.

When Steel finally broke off the kiss it was to lift her up in his arms and sit with her on his lap on the sofa. 'Listen to me, my love,' he said shakily. 'You must try to understand. I can't stop the Barbaras of the world behaving the way they do, but they can't touch us unless you let them. I'm yours, body, soul and spirit and I promise you this day you are enough for me until forever and beyond. I will never give you cause to doubt me, never. You are my sun, moon and stars and I want you as my wife and the mother of my children. And I will teach you to trust, believe me. Until the last shadow of doubt in yourself is gone. When you see yourself as I see you, you will have no need to fear. I want you in sickness and in health, now and in old age. I'll push you in your Bath chair if you'll push me in mine.'

He kissed her again, crushing her willing lips under his, deepening the kiss until finally he sighed, a long desperate sound as he muttered, 'I've been going insane, quietly insane.'

'Oh, Steel. I've been so unhappy,' she cried softly. 'I've wanted you so much but I've been so frightened.'

'No more, my love. No more. I need you every bit as much as you need me. I can't live without you.'

She nuzzled her face into his throat. 'I've missed you so much. And I thought you didn't want me any more.'

He pulled back a little, looking into her flushed face. 'Do you want a big wedding?' he asked thickly.

'A big wedding?' She stared at him, surprised. 'No, no, I don't think so. I did all that before and it was almost impersonal. But—but we've plenty of time before—'

'Good, because I want to marry you soon, next week even. Would you do that? We can get the girls pretty dresses and have your parents and Annie and Jeff, Maggie too.'

'Next week? Can you do that? There's so much red tape.'

'I can do it,' he said firmly. 'Money was made to do away with red tape. I want you, Toni. In my bed, as my wife. I want it to be right from the start. No hole-in-the-wall affair. I've had enough of them in the past. This is different. You're different. We'll come together as man and wife and not till then.'

She felt a moment's panic. Things were happening too fast. And then she looked into Steel's face and saw the love shining out of his eyes.

'I want to love you, Toni. Properly. I want to spend all night showing you how much I love you, and with the best intentions in the world my control only goes so far when we're together like this. And once that ring is on your finger you can't change your mind,' he added, grinning.

She drew in a steadying breath. This still terrified her, but she'd glimpsed a future in which there was no Steel and she couldn't go through that again. She loved him. And with Steel at her side she could learn to trust herself again, to regain what had been eaten away after she'd met Richard.

'So, the shortest engagement in living history?' Steel asked her, only the faintest shadow in his eyes betraying the glimmer of uncertainty he was feeling as to her reaction.

Toni smiled. 'I warn you now, the girls will want pink dresses.'

# EPILOGUE

TEN YEARS HAD PASSED since the snowy February day when Steel had carried his bride over the threshold of the house in Magpie Lane. Ten years of love and laughter and happiness, along with the odd hiccup, which was only to be expected in family life.

Amelia and Daisy were now beautiful young girls on the verge of womanhood, confident and secure as only greatly beloved children could be.

Steel and Toni's son had been born a year after the marriage, and another son had followed within eighteen months. Katie Jane had been born on their fifth wedding anniversary and managed to twist everyone in the household round her little finger from day one. Except perhaps her mother.

Toni watched her youngest daughter now as she played with her brothers in the tree house Steel had constructed at the end of the garden. Even from the patio where they were sitting enjoying the last of the afternoon sunshine, she could hear Katie ordering her long-suffering brothers about.

'She's dreadfully bossy.' Toni turned to Steel beside her. 'You all spoil her outrageously, you know.'

Steel grinned. It still had the power to make her knees weak. She wouldn't have thought he could have grown

more handsome, but family life suited him. The slightly
stern edge to his good looks had mellowed and the result
was more devastating than before. The two boys, Harry
and John, were every bit as handsome as their father,
but Katie Jane took after her. Steel declared she was
beautiful.

She reached out now and took his hand, the desire
that never seemed to wane however much she had of
him strong. 'I love you so much,' she murmured.

'And I you.' He leant across and kissed her and her
blood fizzed. 'For ever and a day.'

She knew that was true now. She had known it for a
long time. Nights spent in their big bed when he spent
hours worshipping her with his hands and mouth and
tongue before taking her to oblivion and back had begun
the process, and his longing to be with her every minute
he could, his adoration of the children—and he regarded
Amelia and Daisy as his—and his pleasure in their home
and life together had finally enabled her to become the
woman she was meant to be.

Shortly after their marriage Steel had drastically reduced the amount of time he was at the office, employ-
ing a chief executive to run the business for him much
of the time. He wanted to be a hands-on father, he'd explained to Toni, and it was important Amelia and Daisy
bonded with him. They had bonded with him so well
that the twins had become proper little Daddy's girls,
but Toni hadn't minded being ousted into second place
now and again. She was just so grateful Steel genuinely
loved the twins as his own and that they regarded him
as their father.

Along with the children the house had been filled
with pets. At present three dogs, two cats, six ham-
sters and a house bunny called Fraser—who ruled the

roost—added to the mayhem. But every day was precious and Toni wouldn't change a thing. Steel had even had a bungalow built in the grounds for her parents two years ago when the stairs at their terrace had become too much for her father. It meant the elderly couple could still have their independence but be part of family life when they chose to be, and both of them—but especially her mother—thought Steel was the best thing since sliced bread.

Toni agreed with them. To be able to go to sleep wrapped in Steel's arms and wake up in the morning and have him make slow, sweet love to her was more precious than gold. She had a beautiful home filled with the sound of children's laughter, five happy, healthy children, but most of all she had Steel. He was hers, all hers, and she knew she was the most important person in the world to him because he told her so every day.

And because he thought she was beautiful, she *was* beautiful, she thought now as he kissed her again. The gremlins of the past had gone. She was whole. She was loved.

0411 Gen Std HB

# MAY 2011
# HARDBACK TITLES

## ROMANCE

| | |
|---|---|
| Too Proud to be Bought | Sharon Kendrick |
| A Dark Sicilian Secret | Jane Porter |
| Prince of Scandal | Annie West |
| The Beautiful Widow | Helen Brooks |
| Strangers in the Desert | Lynn Raye Harris |
| The Ultimate Risk | Chantelle Shaw |
| Sins of the Past | Elizabeth Power |
| A Night With Consequences | Margaret Mayo |
| Cupcakes and Killer Heels | Heidi Rice |
| Sex, Gossip and Rock & Roll | Nicola Marsh |
| Riches to Rags Bride | Myrna Mackenzie |
| Rancher's Twins: Mum Needed | Barbara Hannay |
| The Baby Project | Susan Meier |
| Second Chance Baby | Susan Meier |
| The Love Lottery | Shirley Jump |
| Her Moment in the Spotlight | Nina Harrington |
| Her Little Secret | Carol Marinelli |
| The Doctor's Damsel in Distress | Janice Lynn |

## HISTORICAL

| | |
|---|---|
| Lady Drusilla's Road to Ruin | Christine Merrill |
| Glory and the Rake | Deborah Simmons |
| To Marry a Matchmaker | Michelle Styles |
| The Mercenary's Bride | Terri Brisbin |

## MEDICAL™

| | |
|---|---|
| The Taming of Dr Alex Draycott | Joanna Neil |
| The Man Behind the Badge | Sharon Archer |
| St Piran's: Tiny Miracle Twins | Maggie Kingsley |
| Maverick in the ER | Jessica Matthews |

04011 Gen Std LP

# MAY 2011
# LARGE PRINT TITLES

## ROMANCE

| | |
|---|---|
| Hidden Mistress, Public Wife | Emma Darcy |
| Jordan St Claire: Dark and Dangerous | Carole Mortimer |
| The Forbidden Innocent | Sharon Kendrick |
| Bound to the Greek | Kate Hewitt |
| Wealthy Australian, Secret Son | Margaret Way |
| A Winter Proposal | Lucy Gordon |
| His Diamond Bride | Lucy Gordon |
| Juggling Briefcase & Baby | Jessica Hart |

## HISTORICAL

| | |
|---|---|
| Courting Miss Vallois | Gail Whitiker |
| Reprobate Lord, Runaway Lady | Isabelle Goddard |
| The Bride Wore Scandal | Helen Dickson |
| Chivalrous Captain, Rebel Mistress | Diane Gaston |

## MEDICAL™

| | |
|---|---|
| Dr Zinetti's Snowkissed Bride | Sarah Morgan |
| The Christmas Baby Bump | Lynne Marshall |
| Christmas in Bluebell Cove | Abigail Gordon |
| The Village Nurse's Happy-Ever-After | Abigail Gordon |
| The Most Magical Gift of All | Fiona Lowe |
| Christmas Miracle: A Family | Dianne Drake |

# JUNE 2011
# HARDBACK TITLES

## ROMANCE

| | |
|---|---|
| Passion and the Prince | Penny Jordan |
| For Duty's Sake | Lucy Monroe |
| Alessandro's Prize | Helen Bianchin |
| Mr and Mischief | Kate Hewitt |
| Wife in the Shadows | Sara Craven |
| The Brooding Stranger | Maggie Cox |
| An Inconvenient Obsession | Natasha Tate |
| The Girl He Never Noticed | Lindsay Armstrong |
| The Privileged and the Damned | Kimberly Lang |
| The Big Bad Boss | Susan Stephens |
| Her Desert Prince | Rebecca Winters |
| A Family for the Rugged Rancher | Donna Alward |
| The Boss's Surprise Son | Teresa Carpenter |
| Soldier on Her Doorstep | Soraya Lane |
| Ordinary Girl in a Tiara | Jessica Hart |
| Tempted by Trouble | Liz Fielding |
| Flirting with the Society Doctor | Janice Lynn |
| When One Night Isn't Enough | Wendy S Marcus |

## HISTORICAL

| | |
|---|---|
| Ravished by the Rake | Louise Allen |
| The Rake of Hollowhurst Castle | Elizabeth Beacon |
| Bought for the Harem | Anne Herries |
| Slave Princess | Juliet Landon |

## MEDICAL™

| | |
|---|---|
| Melting the Argentine Doctor's Heart | Meredith Webber |
| Small Town Marriage Miracle | Jennifer Taylor |
| St Piran's: Prince on the Children's Ward | Sarah Morgan |
| Harry St Clair: Rogue or Doctor? | Fiona McArthur |

05011 Gen Std LP

# JUNE 2011
# LARGE PRINT TITLES

## ROMANCE

| | |
|---|---|
| Flora's Defiance | Lynne Graham |
| The Reluctant Duke | Carole Mortimer |
| The Wedding Charade | Melanie Milburne |
| The Devil Wears Kolovsky | Carol Marinelli |
| The Nanny and the CEO | Rebecca Winters |
| Friends to Forever | Nikki Logan |
| Three Weddings and a Baby | Fiona Harper |
| The Last Summer of Being Single | Nina Harrington |

## HISTORICAL

| | |
|---|---|
| Lady Arabella's Scandalous Marriage | Carole Mortimer |
| Dangerous Lord, Seductive Miss | Mary Brendan |
| Bound to the Barbarian | Carol Townend |
| The Shy Duchess | Amanda McCabe |

## MEDICAL™

| | |
|---|---|
| St Piran's: The Wedding of The Year | Caroline Anderson |
| St Piran's: Rescuing Pregnant Cinderella | Carol Marinelli |
| A Christmas Knight | Kate Hardy |
| The Nurse Who Saved Christmas | Janice Lynn |
| The Midwife's Christmas Miracle | Jennifer Taylor |
| The Doctor's Society Sweetheart | Lucy Clark |

WEB/M&B/RTL3 HB

*Discover Pure Reading Pleasure with*

## Visit the Mills & Boon website for all the latest in romance

- 🌹 **Buy** all the latest releases, backlist and eBooks

- 🌹 **Join** our community and chat to authors and other readers

- 🌹 **Win** with our fantastic online competitions

- 🌹 **Tell us** what you think by signing up to our reader panel

- 🌹 **Find out** more about our authors and their books

- 🌹 **Free** online reads from your favourite authors

- 🌹 **Sign** up for our free monthly eNewsletter

- 🌹 **Rate** and review books with our star system

# www.millsandboon.co.uk

 Follow us at twitter.com/millsandboonuk

 Become a fan at facebook.com/romancehq